Glas.

R W Prescott

Glass Fever

Matador
9 De Montfort Mews
Leicester LE1 7FW, UK
Tel: (+44) 116 255 9311 / 9312
Email: books@troubador.co.uk
Web: www.troubador.co.uk/matador

ISBN 1 904744 22 2

Cover illustration: Troubador / Photos.com

Typeset in 12pt Plantin by Troubador Publishing Ltd, Leicester, UK

Matador is an imprint of Troubador Publishing

Printed and bound by The Cromwell Press, Trowbridge, Wiltshire.

Contents

1	Orange Treacle	1
2	Glass Swan	9
3	Lemonade Bottle	19
4	Crystal Ball	29
5	Flamingo Woman	38
6	Welsh Chapel	47
7	Glass Goblet	55
8	Walking a Tightrope	61
9	The Bacchus Vase	69
10	Sixpenny Spectacles	78
11	Glass Fish	87
12	In the Limelight	95
13	Our Emma	105

Chapter 1

Orange Treacle

At the canal bridge, Emma put down her bundle and unbuttoned her scruffy old boots, shaking out the grit and resting her sore feet. She stared through the murky haze which covered the town of Clayminster. All around her, rows of factory chimneys belched smoke into the air, and straight ahead loomed the biggest chimney of all, shaped like a massive cone and protected by a circle of high walls. A loud wail from the factory hooter made her jump like a scared rabbit.

Quickly fastening her boots, she picked up her bundle and hurried across the cobble-stoned bridge. In front of her stood a tall archway, carrying the name of the factory in big, proud letters: HARDSHAWS PLATE GLASSWORKS. A steam engine chugged alongside the walls and passed under the archway, pulling a line of wagons piled with sand.

'Watch out there!' shouted a man, coming from behind the arch. He wore a top hat and a frock coat, a posh gentleman in Emma's eyes. 'You shouldn't be here, lass!'

She would have gladly run off, but she had an errand to finish. 'I've brought dinner snap for George and John.'

'George and John? We must have a hundred

Georges and five hundred Johns.'

'I mean George and John Peaseley.'

'Ah, the Peaseleys.' The man scratched his bushy whiskers, a peppery mixture of brown and grey. 'They're in the Great Casting Hall. John's a glass blower now. Good lad, he is, too.'

'I know,' said Emma. She could feel a blush travelling up her face like the flame on a gas lamp.

John was her favourite in the family. Aged twenty-two, he was tall and broad-shouldered, with a mischievous smile. He always had a kind word for her, unlike the others. Whenever she blushed at home, they laughed at her for having a red face to match her red hair, but John called it red-gold hair, which sounded much better.

'All right, come with me,' said the man. 'We'll find them, and you can see inside the Great Casting Hall, the biggest in the land, two hundred yards long and fifty yards wide.'

'Please, mister, can't you take their snap for me?'

'Nay, I'm not dinner-fetcher round here. Come on, you'll learn a thing or two.'

He led her across a courtyard and under a second archway, where a monstrous building, bigger than a church, rose up in front of her. Often she'd seen the dark, grim hall from a distance, but never close up like this, towering above her like a volcano. Smoke was pumping from ventilators in the roof, and a terrific heat was blasting from the doorway.

Some girls at school said it was a prison for fire-breathing dragons, all bursting to get out. Emma hung back, afraid of being burnt alive, but the man gave a reassuring smile and ushered her inside.

The vast interior made her eyes shoot everywhere. No dragons, but high pointed arches, supported by massive brick pillars, stretched far into the distance, till you could hardly see the last ones. The clang of machinery and the shouts of the workers echoed down the massive chamber. Near the entrance, three huge bins nearly reached the ceiling, and men were loading sand into one of them. Further on, the dark recesses of the hall were lit by flashes of fire from a giant oven.

'Yon furnace is eighty feet long,' said the whiskery man. 'Watch the molten glass when it comes out. It's just like orange treacle.'

The noise and the heat were shaking Emma, but she perked up when she saw John Peaseley approach the furnace and draw out a great gob of orange treacle, using the end of a long blowpipe.

With his cheeks puffed out like cricket balls, he blew down the pipe till the molten lump slowly ballooned into a cylinder of glass, a good five feet in length. Sweat was gushing off his face, and he seemed like some hero of old, fighting the orange treacle dragon and throwing it on the table, where the labourers sliced it down the middle and rolled it flat.

'Beer!' shouted John. 'Fetch some beer, will you?'

A boy, not much older than Emma, ran from the side of the hall and handed John a tankard of beer, which he downed in one go.

'It's thirsty work,' said the man, 'and the beer helps the stomach, with all these fumes around. The men get beer as part of their payment. Good idea, eh?'

'Don't they all get drunk?' said Emma. More than once she'd seen George Peaseley rolling home merry and falling asleep at the kitchen table.

'They soon sweat it out of them,' said the man. 'Hey, John, here's your lass wi' dinner snap!'

John looked up and smiled when he saw Emma. He took off the protective leather gloves he was wearing, and wiped his brow with a rag. On his arms were bands of leather to give more protection, but his shirt was torn here and there, showing cuts and burns.

'Now then, our Emma,' he said.

She liked that – 'our Emma'. He was the only one who called her that, because she didn't really belong to the Peaseley family. They'd taken her from the workhouse two years ago, at the age of nine. Officially she was a foster child, but they only wanted her as an unpaid servant. This morning, what with all her other chores, she hadn't got the snap ready in time, and the men had to leave without it.

John took the bundle from Emma and nodded respectfully at the man. 'Thanks, Mr Hardshaw. It was kind of thee to let her in.'

Emma's jaw dropped. The man in the top hat, so friendly and ordinary, was the famous Mr Hardshaw, who seemed to own half of Clayminster, including the colliery and the brickworks, as well as the glassworks.

'That's no bother,' said Mr Hardshaw. 'I've a lad at home just about her age. P'raps I'll swap him for her. He's a real nuisances, always in trouble, ever since I sent him to that boarding school down south.'

He pulled a pocket watch from his waistcoat and gave it a quick glance. 'I must be off now. Meeting with the board of directors. We're into new plans, John. I'm looking for a continuous flow of metal, twenty-four hours a day, and no waiting for batches of it. Soon Hardshaws will be the biggest and best glassmakers in the world. See your lass gets out safely, eh? Bye, young miss.'

Emma stammered a good bye and looked confused. She turned to John.

'I thought you made glass, not metal,' she said.

'That's what we call molten glass, we call it metal.'

'Orange treacle makes more sense.'

John laughed and led her away from the scorching heat of the giant furnace. He shouted for his stepfather George, who came from behind a pillar, clutching a tankard of beer.

'Sithee, here's our Emma wi' dinner snap.'

'What's she doin' inside 'ere?' said George.

'Mr Hardshaw let her in,' said John.

'Well, I'll be a monkey's uncle,' said George. His bald head glistened like a polished dome and he wore a thick leather belt around an ample stomach. He was chewing tobacco, and spat some brown froth on the floor, right in front of Emma.

'We can't have thee bothering Mr Hardshaw,' he said. 'You'd better get our snap ready on time, or I'll be taking my belt to thee.'

'No you won't,' said John.

'Listen to Lord Muck,' muttered George, 'just because he's a glass-blower and hobnobs with the likes of Mr Hardshaw. Remember, my lad, pride comes afore a fall.'

On his heavy clogs, he clumped along the side of the hall and reached a group of women who were smoothing and polishing panes of glass, ready for dispatch through the far end of the building. He spoke to one of them, who looked down the hall towards Emma, pointing and laughing. It was Madge, the older Peaseley girl, and her jeering voice cut through the noise of the furnace.

'Hey, Gingernut, still looking for yer mam and dad?'

The colour rushed to Emma's face, as several workmen turned in her direction. She believed with all her heart that her parents were still alive, but made the mistake of blurting this out from time to time. People just smiled, or in Madge's case, found new ammunition for teasing. She turned on her heel and made for the door.

Don't cry, she told herself, Madge only wants to see you cry. Anyway, what does she know? Your parents are alive, aren't they? She stumbled, and John caught her by the arm.

'Hey, take no notice of her,' he said. 'Come on, it's my break, and I'll show thee how to make a frigger.'

'I'll be late for school,' she said.

'It won't take long,' he said. 'We've just finished this batch of metal, and there's a little left over. We're allowed to make things for ourselves, you know, little glass ornaments and suchlike.'

With his blowpipe, John drew some orange treacle

from the giant furnace and blew gently till the molten glass swelled into a hollow ball. Using pincers, he spun out a long neck, and then heated the glass again. After bending and shaping it into a body, he marked the surface delicately with a knife, this side and that.

There, right in front of her, Emma saw a perfect glass swan being born, with an elegant curved neck and finely-feathered wings.

A cry of wonder came from her lips. 'Eh-h-h!' she said. 'That's proper magic!'

'We must cool it slowly,' said John, 'or it'll break into many pieces. That's glass, see? Strong and beautiful, but weak and fragile, just like thee, little Emma.'

Neatly and swiftly, he snapped the glass swan from the end of the blowpipe and placed it inside a small oven nearby. From the furnace, he picked up another dollop of orange treacle.

'Is there owt else you'd like me to make?'

'A ship,' she said instantly.

'Eh-up, Emma, that's a tough 'un!'

But he went straight into it, blowing and pulling and twisting, adding smaller blobs, gluing pieces of glass together, and working delicately with the pincers, like a magician conjuring a shape from thin air.

Gradually, a ship appeared, shining brightly with mast and sails, fore and aft. Hundreds of tiny lights sparkled around the rigging, and Emma thought she could see the sails moving in a slight breeze. If only she could travel on a ship like that, sailing to some far-off land and joining her parents on a sunlit shore.

All at once, the glass ship spiralled upwards,

gaining a wooden deck and brass fittings and canvas sails, growing into a fully-rigged schooner, which swept Emma aboard and sailed through the walls of the Great Casting Hall like they were flimsy clouds of mist. She rushed to the side-rail and watched in amazement as the ship splashed into the muddy waters of the Clayminster canal and headed downstream.

She had another shock, when she looked at her clothes. Gone were her pinafore and mob cap. Instead she was wearing a white muslin dress and a straw hat with ribbons. On her feet, a brand-new pair of button-boots were polished to a fine sheen.

Skimming along to the end of the canal, the schooner entered a fast-flowing river, so broad that Emma could hardly see the other side. The sky became a clear blue and a fresh wind blew on her face. Now she felt excited, like she never had before, as if facing some adventure or preparing to meet some important person.

The towers and cranes of a busy port came into view. This must be Ravenpool, thought Emma, where sea-voyages began, to the Americas and beyond.

When her ship laid anchor, people crowded the docks to wave her good-bye, and a little boat came out with a passenger on board, ready to join her. As the boat drew nearer, Emma could see the passenger clearly. She was a pretty woman in a gown of pink satin and a broad-brimmed floral hat. Steps were lowered and she came on deck, making straight for Emma. She had a warm smile and twinkling blue eyes. Her voice was soft and gentle.

'Hello, Emma,' she said. 'I'm your mother.'

Chapter 2

Glass Swan

Sparkling diamonds shone around her mother's head and Emma tried to reach out and touch her, but the scene evaporated into a mist and she was back in the noise and dust of the Great Casting Hall, her hands only inches away from the glowing ship.

'Watch out!' said John. 'She's not ready yet. You can have a frigger from last week's batch, to tide you over.'

'John, I've just seen my mam!' said Emma, but he was too busy placing the ship in the oven to catch her words.

The pillars of the Great Casting Hall spun around her and she was dizzy with excitement. She wanted to be back on the ship, getting to know her mother, but John was in front of her, carrying a rack full of little glass animals and birds.

'Normally I'd sell 'em at the market,' he said, 'but you can have first choice.'

Emma tried hard to concentrate. She liked them all, including a cat, a mouse, and an owl, but she saw a swan, like the one he'd made first, and chose that. John presented it to her with a mock bow.

'There we are, your ladyship! A good luck charm for thee.'

Emma curtsied back and took the swan in her trembling hands. She nearly dropped it as the hooter sounded its wailing note again, echoing loudly down the hall. John said it meant another batch of metal was ready for blowing, and gave Emma a rag to wrap around the swan. He walked with her as far as the main entrance, where she waved good-bye and returned to the world outside, her head spinning with all she had seen.

Till now, her parents had been shadowy figures who drifted in and out of her dreams, but the glass ship had given her power to see her mother bright and clear.

She must be alive. Where was she now? How could she find her? And where was her father?

The sticky atmosphere clogged her brain and made it difficult to think straight. Poisonous fumes poured into the air from the glassworks, the chemical works, the brickworks, and the copper smelting works. The worst smell of all came from the chemical works, a stench like rotten eggs, which made Emma's nostrils curl.

Hot and sweaty under her long skirt, she stopped at the canal bridge, where some bargemen were unloading coal. Steam was rising gently from the filthy encrusted surface of the water. On the opposite bank stood a new clock tower, and she was shocked to see the time. Ten to nine! She was late for school again and her hands were already sore from the vicious blows of the leather strap. She wondered whether to twag it, but remembered the school attendance officer, who was ruthless in patrolling the streets.

'Run for it,' she told herself, 'you'll have to run for it!'

Over the cobbled bridge she clattered, her heavy skirt swishing around her ankles and holding her back. As she reached the other side, her foot caught in the hem and she fell forwards, her precious package tumbling from her hands. The bright crystal swan rolled out of the rag and onto the cobblestones.

'No!' cried Emma.

She scooped the bird up and cradled it in both hands. To her relief, nothing was broken. She stroked the neck, and diamonds seem to sparkle beneath the feathers. If I were a swan, thought Emma, I'd never be late for school or ever get the strap. I'd fly there every day.

Suddenly the glass bird gave a warm heart-beat, growing warmer and louder, and Emma held her breath as the wings began to move and the glass became feathers and the feathers swept around her like a snowstorm, and she was dwindling in size, with the odd sensation of her toes gluing together and her neck curving round.

The flurry of movement ended. She looked down and saw two webbed feet and her body covered in pure white plumage. When she tried to move her arms, a pair of giant wings unfolded.

Panic seized hold of her. She tried to shout 'help', but only a hissing noise came out of her orange-coloured beak. What had she done, turning herself into a swan just to get to school on time? She appeared all fine and elegant, as if wearing new clothes, but her swan's heart thumped in a frenzy as she wondered what to do next.

Flying was the answer, but how? Swans took off from water, something she'd seen in the park, but that was on a clear lake, not a canal full of dangerous sludge which might drag her down.

She had no other option. Terrified, she dropped over the side and splashed frantically through the slime. On the canal banks, she could hear the bargemen shouting as she raced past them. Her feet thrashed the water and her wings beat the air, but she couldn't lift herself up from the cloggy surface.

Why couldn't she fly? If she didn't take off soon, she'd hit the next bridge. She hissed at herself in anger.

All of a sudden her legs flattened against her body, the water released its hold, and her flapping wings lifted her skywards. She felt so light and yet so strong, without a hot clammy skirt to hold her back. Her fears fell away, like the canal beneath, and she soared upwards through the smelly murk of Clayminster into the cooler, fresher air.

Over the brewery and the brickworks she flew, and the yellow clouds of the chemical works, watching the chimneys and cones and slag-heaps dwindle to a toy size. Down below, through gaps in the haze, she could see rows and rows of grimy terraced houses. One of them was number 9, Clarence Street, where she scrubbed and cleaned and cooked for the Peaseleys, but they couldn't boss her around up here, not where she was mistress of a clear blue sky. She was free, free to fly anywhere she wanted!

With her swan's eye view, she might even find her parents, but where would she start? Doubts began to creep into her mind. What if she ended up circling the sky in a futile search? And when she landed, would she stay a swan forever, or become Emma once again?

She would have to make a decision and quickly. Her powerful swan-wings had already carried her to the edge of the crowded town, where she could see the railway line heading north and the twin buildings of Field Street Elementary School.

The ordinary life below, full of the unexpected but containing her only hope, pulled her earthwards like a magnet. Down she swooped and her stomach rolled over as she descended towards the girls' entrance, landing on two feet outside the gates and shedding her feathers and wings, just as her teacher, Miss Plews, was ringing the hand-bell in the yard.

Two miles in two minutes, and Emma was shaking with excitement at her flight. The glass swan was back in her hands, warm inside the rag, and she held it close as she lined up with the rest of the girls.

'Where've you been?' whispered Mary Meaney, her friend from Clarence Street. 'I was waiting for you on the corner.'

'I had to go to Hardshaws, and John gave me a glass swan, and I've flown through the sky, honest I have.'

With a stony glare, Miss Plews silenced any further conversation, and the girls moved inside their

13

grim classroom, with its high ceiling and tall desk for the teacher. Emma found a place on one of the long benches, crammed in with fifty other girls of the 'senior class'.

Miss Plews stared at the package in Emma's hand. 'What's that you have?' she said.

'Miss, it's a glass swan, a present from my foster-brother.'

'Give it to me. I shall confiscate it till home time. You know the rules, you disobedient girl!'

Watching her swan disappear into a cupboard, Emma bit her lip in frustration. In front of her, a girl turned round and sniggered, a large girl with big teeth like a horse. She was Hannah Tunstall, whose father had the local grocer's shop. Their family was rich enough to afford two servants, which made Hannah look down on people like Emma.

'Scruffy little Peaseley,' she said. 'You'll never see your toy again and they'll send you back to the workhouse!'

Emma flinched and tried to say something back, but Miss Plews started the morning prayers. After a hymn, she chalked the date on the blackboard, *Friday, 8th July, 1881*, and dictated a passage for the girls to write down in their books. At the end, they had to queue up to show her their efforts. Some girls received the strap for slovenly writing, and poor Mary ended up in the corner wearing the dunce's cap.

When Miss Plews grudgingly ticked her work, Emma seized her chance.

'Miss, can I have my swan back now?'

'Don't be impertinent,' said her teacher, 'or you'll never get it back!'

As she returned to her bench, Emma passed the cupboard where the swan lay. She put her mouth close to the wooden door. 'Don't worry,' she whispered. 'You'll be all right.'

Yet nothing was safe that day, not even in Field Street Elementary School. In the next lesson, the senior girls had to chant a long list of kings and queens, and they'd just reached Henry the Eighth when a brick came crashing through the window and landed at the side of Miss Plews. She screamed and crouched behind her desk, white-faced and trembling.

The girls scattered in different directions, while Emma scrambled towards the cupboard to protect her glass swan. Through the broken window, she could hear a familiar voice receding into the distance, drunken and slurred, shouting 'Up the Workers' Revolutionary Union!' and 'Down with all tyrants!'

Was it him? Could he really do a thing like that? She hurried across the room and saw a tall figure retreating down Field Street. Her heart sank. It was him all right, it was Alfred Peaseley, as large as life, John's older brother.

The headmaster burst in and bawled at Emma to come away from the window. He told the pupil teacher to fetch the police, and advised Miss Plews to give the girls some drill to calm them down, while the caretaker cleaned up the mess. Out in the yard, Miss Plews recovered her composure and marched her girls up and down in pairs, despite the oppressive heat.

The local 'bobby', PC Fossett, arrived, and Emma smiled when she saw him. He was small for a policeman, with a big black beard, like the picture of a prophet on the classroom wall, and his tunic had brass buttons all the way up the middle. Perched on his head, his helmet seemed about to fall off.

Miss Plews ordered everyone back into the classroom to have their dinner. In her rush to take the snap to the factory, Emma had forgotten hers and gratefully received some of Mary's, an iron-hard crust of bread covered in dripping.

PC Fossett addressed them. 'Now then, young ladies, did any of you see the villains who broke this 'ere window?'

Emma felt herself going red, but stayed very still. Mary looked at her, Hannah Tunstall looked at her, Miss Plews looked at her, and she was sure PC Fossett was looking at her, then to her horror Hannah put her hand up.

'Yes, young miss?'

'Sir, they were shouting something about the Workers' Pollution.'

'You mean the Workers' Revolution,' said Miss Plews.

'That'll be the Workers' Revolutionary Union,' said PC Fossett. 'Thank you, young miss. I've a fair idea who the culprit might be.'

'Hannah Tunstall,' said Miss Plews, 'I shall award you a gold star for your keen observation.'

Hannah flicked her hair back and preened herself. Smugly content, she turned and leered at Emma.

When PC Fossett left, Miss Plews started a geography lesson, using a large globe to show the spread of the British Empire.

'See, our colonies are all in red,' she said. 'Our glorious monarch, Queen Victoria, rules a quarter of the world, as far as you can see. The sun never sets on the British Empire.'

She spun the globe and pointed to Australia. In her mind's eye, Emma was already crossing the oceans, with the wind on her face, to a new land on the far side of the world, sailing with her mother, like she had in the glass ship, and with her father as the captain.

'And what is the name of the country below Australia, these two islands here?' asked Miss Plews.

Emma's hand shot up and Miss Plews looked at her in surprise.

'Miss, it's New Zealand, North and South Island.'

'Er, yes – correct.'

Emma waited for a gold star, but didn't get one. Hannah looked across, angry that she couldn't answer before Emma. She was even angrier during embroidery, when Emma stitched a better napkin than she did. When school ended, Emma finally collected her glass swan, but not without another scolding from Miss Plews.

Outside, Hannah Tunstall and her gang were waiting in the school yard. Mary Meaney shouted a warning, as Hannah strode forward, her eyes full of spite.

'What've you got there, Peaseley? Give it to me.'

Too late, Emma hid the swan behind her back, and Hannah gripped her arms till they hurt. When Mary tried to intervene, she was quickly pushed away by other members of the gang. After a hard struggle, Hannah wrestled the bundle from Emma and uncovered the dazzling glass bird.

'Well, look at that! It's far too nice for a scruffy servant girl like you. Oh dear, I've dropped it.'

With a grand gesture, Hannah flung the swan into the air and Emma prayed for it to fly away, but down it came, smashing onto the concrete and breaking into a thousand pieces.

Chapter 3

Lemonade Bottle

Emma stared in disbelief at her beautiful swan, scattered around the yard in glittering splinters. Pin-pricks of pain ran through her body, like she was breaking into little bits herself. She picked up part of a wing and held it out, waiting for the exhilarating lift into the air, but it wouldn't fly, it wouldn't do anything. Anger welled up inside her and she was about to rush at Hannah, when Miss Plews came out and shouted her name.

'Emma Peaseley, look at the mess you've made. You are a disgrace. Go and get a dustpan and brush and clean this lot up.'

'Miss, it was Hannah who done it,' said Mary.

'I was just on my way out, miss,' said Hannah.

'Of course you were,' said Miss Plews. 'Off you go, and give my regards to your father. He's by far the best grocer in town.'

Emma saw it was a waste of time trying to tell the truth and went for the dustpan and brush. Mary helped her sweep up the pieces, and as they dropped the glass into the bin, Emma felt herself being dragged down into a dark hole.

'It was a magic swan,' she said.

'I didn't really see it,' said Mary.

'It gave me wings and I flew here this morning, cross my heart and hope to die.'

'Hush your face,' said Mary, 'or they'll put you in a loony bin. Come on, we'll go for a paddle in the Steamies.'

Emma sighed. The Steamies were a long way off, across the town centre and back towards the canal bridge, from where she'd flown on her swan-wings.

Luckily, as they reached the end of Field Street, a horse-drawn tram passed by and slowed down to take on passengers. They jumped on board and travelled several streets before the conductor threw them off for having no money.

By the time they reached the Steamies they were footsore and weary. It was a favourite bathing spot for Clayminster children, where the glassworks drew water from the canal to cool its furnaces, and pumped it back warm and steaming. They took off their boots and stockings and paddled in the warm water, and for a while it was peaceful, watching the barges carrying coal down to the river.

As she looked down into the Steamies, Emma saw the bright colours of tropical fish, thrown there by a pet shop owner who'd gone bankrupt. They thrived in the warm conditions, and made Emma dream she was in Africa or India, living with her parents in some outpost of the British Empire.

Something nibbled her toe. With a cry, she jumped to her feet and glanced at the clock on the tower.

'Come on, Mary. We'd best get moving or I'll be in more trouble.'

They dried their feet with their stockings and hurried bare-footed along the canal bank. At Victoria Road, which was busy with traffic, they put on their boots and soggy stockings, and ran to the corner where Tunstalls had their grocer's shop. Legs of ham were hung up outside, and the window was full of bottles and jars.

'How about getting our own back on the Tunstalls?' said Mary. 'Let's pinch some toffee.'

'No,' said Emma. 'A girl got seven days' prison for stealing bread last week.'

'Don't worry,' said Mary. 'They'll never catch me. Keep a look-out, will you?'

Emma was left gazing through the window, unwilling to help a thief, but unable to leave a friend. The heat and dust of Clayminster gave her a terrible thirst, and a row of lemonade bottles tempted her to look deeper into their dark green glass. One of the bottles began to burst with light, and she trembled in anticipation as the bubbles turned into sparkling diamonds.

As slippery as quicksilver, she poured through the window and into the green-shaded world of the bottle, where she floated and drank all she wanted from a sea of lemonade. The bottle emptied, like a tide receding, and immediately quenched her thirst, but when she tried to move, she was shocked to find her skin had turned into green glass and her red-gold hair into a cork.

How could she get out of the bottle and back into her own body? She'd no legs to walk on, just a wobbly base, and no hands to push the cork out, just little green shoulders. She screamed, but she had no voice, just bubbles and air.

Her glass skin was sweating with fear and drips of lemonade began to trickle down her neck. She was trapped in Tunstall's shop, and all her life she'd be filled with lemonade and emptied into glasses, over and over again! Her only chance was to be broken into pieces and melted into something else, but that might never happen. Why didn't she stay a glass swan? Now she'd never find her parents.

Through a green mist, she saw Mary helping herself to some liquorice sticks while the assistant climbed a ladder to the top shelf. Suddenly Mr Tunstall came out of his back room and chased her across the sawdust floor. Mary shot through the door, and Mr Tunstall followed her, shouting down the street. When he returned empty-handed, Emma sighed a bubble of relief.

Hannah Tunstall came into the shop, and asked what had happened.

'Some scruffy girl stealing liquorice,' said Mr Tunstall. 'I didn't recognise her.'

'I bet it was Emma Peaseley,' said Hannah. 'She's always in trouble at school.'

'That's what comes of taking in dirty little orphans,' said Mr Tunstall.

Inside her bottle, Emma fizzed and popped with anger. As if hearing something, Mr Tunstall stared at his shelf of lemonade.

'There's an empty bottle there,' he said. 'Hannah,

have you been drinking lemonade behind my back?'

'No, papa, no.'

'You'd better not. Here, put it in the yard.'

Grumbling to herself, Hannah took the bottled Emma into the yard and left her in a crate with some other empties.

The hot July sun burst through the haze and bathed the bottles in a warm glow. Emma felt her blood returning and her heart beating inside the green glass. Her body filled out, the cork shot from the bottle, and in one swift sliding movement she burst from the glass, like a genie from a lamp.

Overjoyed to be herself again, with hands and feet and proper skin, she dashed down a back alley to the Peaseley house in Clarence Street. Inside the kitchen, the children were waiting for her, little Becky and William, aged two and four.

Becky grabbed her skirt and shouted 'Memma', her pet name for her, from when she first tried to say 'Emma'. She rushed to get their tea, some bread and jam, while their mother, Mrs Hetty Peaseley, just sat there lifeless in a chair.

'Where've you been, Emma?' she said. 'The bairns have been driving me up the wall. I feel right jiggered and I'm coming over all mazey, it's so hot. Fetch my pills, quick!'

From the dresser, Emma brought her a box labelled 'Dr Pierce's Purgative Pills', which carried a boast that *No Female should be without them, as a Few Doses carry off all Gross Humours and open all Obstructions*. In Hetty's case, they did not seem to be working.

The jobs piled up on Emma. After the children ate their tea, with jam all over the place, she had to take them to the ashpit privy at the bottom of the yard. The soil-men hadn't been round to empty the pit and the smell hit her as she opened the wooden door. From a tap in the yard, she filled a bucket and took it inside to wash the children. Only a few houses had bathrooms in Clayminster.

George and John Peaseley came in, and sat down at the kitchen table, waiting for their supper. Hetty didn't lift a finger, leaving Emma to serve them some broth, which was bubbling on the grate above the coal fire.

After washing the bairns in a tin bath, she let them play a while, but they began to scramble around the table, and George shouted at Emma to take them upstairs. These two were children from his marriage to Hetty, but John and the others came from Hetty's previous marriage to a chemical worker, who was killed in a works explosion.

Emma took the children upstairs, where they shared a bedroom with herself and Madge, and put them in their little bed, top to tail. When she came down, their mother was busy telling George what an awful day she'd had.

'Aye, well, you'll have a nice day out to-morrow,' said George. 'It's the annual works outing, remember. I might even treat thee to a port and lemon.'

'Oh George, that'll be just up my street,' said Hetty. 'I'll have to build up my strength, though. A little broth should do the trick.'

With a sigh, Emma served her some broth, and had to find another plate when Madge came in, sniffing the air like a hungry bloodhound. Aged eighteen, she was a tall strapping girl, with mean-looking eyes and pale skin.

'Where's our Alfred?' she said.

'Upstairs,' said Hetty. 'He's not feeling very well.'

'PC Fossett wants to see him at the back gate,' said Madge. 'He says he threw a brick through the school window this morning.'

'Well, he were always very headstrong,' said Hetty.

'I'll have a word with Charlie Fossett,' said George. 'Too big for his boots, that's what he is. His father were only a coal miner and now he thinks he can bother decent folk at supper time.'

George clumped out of the kitchen and Emma could hear a heated argument starting in the yard. At the table, Madge was talking about the works' outing and whether any nice-looking boys were going. She was desperate for a husband, especially a well-paid one.

Emma busied herself cutting some bread to go with the broth, but Madge soon remembered she was there.

'My bed linen needs a wash,' she said. 'Gingernut can do it to-morrow, while we're on the works outing.'

Emma took a deep breath. 'I'm goin' as well,' she said.

'You're not goin',' said Madge. 'You've got the house to clean and the bairns to look after.'

'Mam said I could go this time,' said Emma.

'I don't remember,' said Hetty. 'If I did, I must have been flustered.'

'But you promised,' said Emma, 'and I've never been to the sea-side before.'

Madge's hand flashed out and slapped her across the cheek. 'Don't you speak to mam like that,' she said. 'Any more lip and we'll send you back to the workhouse.'

Emma recoiled from the table, dropping some bread on the floor. John stood up and grabbed Madge by the wrist.

'There's no call for that,' he said. 'Emma works hard enough as it is.'

'Yer little favourite, isn't she?' said Madge. 'See what she's done? She's put our mam into a faint.'

With a moan, Hetty reached for Dr Pierce's Purgative Pills.

'Emma doesn't have to miss the trip,' said John. 'We'll take the bairns.'

'I'm not looking after them,' said Madge. 'They might dirty my dress.'

'Catherine will help,' said John.

'Catherine Meaney?' screeched Madge. 'You're not still going out with her, are you? She's just after your money.'

'She's a fine lass,' said John.

'Mam, did you hear that?'

But 'mam' was too busy taking her pills. After a good dosage, she beckoned to Madge, who helped her out of the kitchen, taking care to kick some bread in Emma's direction. Emma wasn't going to cry, that would please Madge too much, but her face was burning from the slap. She bent down to collect the pieces, and John came over to help her.

'Cheer up,' he said. 'You'll get to the seaside. Did you like thy glass swan?'

'Ye-es,' stammered Emma.

What could she tell him? That it was smashed to pieces and lying in a dustbin at the school? She wanted to tell him about her voyage on the ship, her magical swan flight, and her life as a lemonade bottle, but would he believe her? He might think she was a witch, and she'd read somewhere that witches were burnt at the stake.

She heard a cry and went upstairs to check on the children. Becky was awake, which was no wonder, since George and PC Fossett could be heard shouting in the yard.

'You've no proof it were Albert,' said George.

'I shall be watching him,' said PC Fossett. 'You've got a right villain on your hands.'

'Get off my property!' thundered George.

Becky began to whimper and Emma went over to tuck her in. The little girl's forehead felt clammy in the heat of the summer's evening, and the muggy air seemed heavy with impending disaster.

Emma sat on the bed and thought over the weird events of that day. Glass was giving her a strange power, or was it a sickness, something she'd caught in the Great Casting Hall? Clayminster had enough diseases flying around, like typhoid, cholera, and scarlet fever, when people saw things and imagined things. What had she got? A glass fever?

She felt scared, wondering where it would all lead, but curious, wanting to see more of her mother and hopefully her father. Would glass lead her to them?

Chapter 4
Crystal Ball

Early next morning, the glassworkers and their families crowded into Clayminster station and filled the platform for Sandhaven, the seaside resort where Mr Hardshaw took them every summer in a special train. Everybody was dressed in their best clothes, the women in white blouses and flowery hats, the men in waistcoats and straw boaters. Emma had to wear the same old pinafore and mob cap, but standing on a railway platform was adventure enough.

When the train pounded into the station, with steam hissing loudly from its engine, she jumped back in alarm and pulled the children behind her. She gawped at the first class carriage, which was painted white and gold and had leather seats inside. Wearing his silk top hat, Mr Hardshaw stepped forward and escorted on board a beautiful woman in a cream-coloured gown, with a smart bustle at the back.

'That's Mrs Hardshaw,' said John. 'Her dress must have cost a bob or two.'

A nanny in a white starched pinafore followed the Hardshaws into the carriage, leading two toddlers who were like the youngest Peaseleys, but dressed more finely in velvet and lace. Two older boys jumped in after them, one about Emma's age, who wore knickerbockers and waved cheekily at the crowd, and another a few years younger, who had a sailor suit and a peevish look on his face.

Behind them was a tall woman dressed in black, who sniffed the early morning air like a vulture looking for a meal. She stared around the platform and her cruel eyes fixed on Emma, who shrank back among the crowd. The woman hovered for a while, then joined the Hardshaws. I wouldn't like to travel with her, thought Emma.

The glassworkers made a rush for the remaining carriages, which were nearly all third-class with hard wooden seats. Emma sat with the children near a window.

'It's not fair,' said Madge. 'I should be allowed in the second class carriage. It's got velvet seats and rich-looking men.'

'Where's our Alfred?' said George.

'Happen he's gone playing bowls,' said Hetty.

The train steamed out of the station and gathered speed, gradually leaving the rows of dark chimneys for the green and yellow fields of the countryside. The older Peaseleys sat back and George had a sleep, but they'd all been on a train before, unlike Emma, who relished every minute, the clickety-clack of the wheels, the scenery flashing past, and the many little stations along the way. Nothing could replace her lost swan, but her first journey on a train helped to make up for it.

On arriving at Sandhaven, the first class passengers were taken to the beach by horse and carriage. The rest had to walk, and a hot trail it was, especially for the small and feeble. Hetty nearly fainted, but George took her inside a public house and told the other Peaseleys to go on ahead. As they crossed a wide avenue of elegant shops, Madge stopped with a friend to gaze at the latest fashions and was soon left behind. Up a narrow road from here, the glassworkers came to the brow of a hill and Emma gasped at her first view of the sea, gently rolling into a wide expanse of beach, with not a chimney in sight.

The sky was clear, the blue waters stretched for miles, and the sands were dotted with people. Families were sat down as if in their own living room, the women with knitting on their laps and the men smoking pipes and reading their newspapers. A few children were paddling in the water, but nobody else had removed one item of clothing. John brought some chairs over.

'Everything's free,' he said, 'courtesy o' Mr Hardshaw.'

Some donkeys ambled by and the Peaseley bairns screamed with delight when they saw them. John and his girl-friend Catherine helped them onto a donkey each, and escorted the tiny riders off along the sands. Emma walked behind them, wishing she could have a ride herself.

The donkeys had nearly reached the turning point, when she saw the Hardshaw family, gathered near a company of minstrels. The nanny, a young pretty woman, was helping the little ones have a paddle, while their mother reclined gracefully beneath a white parasol. At her side, Mr Hardshaw was singing away happily to the minstrels' songs. Behind them sat the stern woman in black, reading a book. Well away from her, the two Hardshaw boys were playing in the sand.

The donkeys turned around, but Emma lingered a while, curious to observe the family. They looked so well dressed and prosperous. She wondered what would it be like, belonging to them and being called 'Emma Hardshaw' That sounded nice, but 'Lady Emma Hardshaw', that sounded even better!

Not everyone was happy in the Hardshaw camp. The older boy, busy digging in the sand, tried to bury the younger one up to his neck, but he ran crying to the woman in black. She shouted at his brother, who wandered off, looking sullen and bored. He picked up a cricket bat and slammed a ball high into the air. Down it came, straight towards Emma, and she made the neatest catch of her life. He smiled and ran over.

'Good show!' he said. 'I didn't know girls could catch like that.'

She threw the ball back at him, so fiercely it bounced off his chest and onto the sand. Stuck-up posh boy! She turned to follow the donkeys.

'Don't go,' he said. 'I didn't mean to offend you.'

He hurried alongside her, and she stole a glance at him. On his blond head, he wore a flat cap, a grey colour to match his knickerbockers and jacket. A velvet collar gave him a gentlemanly air, but couldn't hide his cheeky grin.

'Would you like to go to the fair?' he said. 'They've

got freaks and roundabouts and the Big Wheel and a circus with dogs and monkeys. It's all free, you've only got to show your Hardshaws' badge.'

'I can't go to the fair,' said Emma, 'and besides, I haven't got a badge.'

'Mine's good enough for two,' he said. 'Quick, before Old Battleaxe sees me.'

'Who's Old Battleaxe?' she asked.

'Madame Renoir, the governess, sat there all in black like a horrid old witch. Last summer, she caught me watching the Fireproof Lady and the Learned Pig.'

They reached the donkey station, where the others had already arrived. John Peaseley came over to them.

'Now then,' he said. 'Who is this young man?'

'I'm Luke Hardshaw,' said the boy.

'Well, I didn't recognise thee, Master Luke,' said John. 'You've grown a bit since I saw thee last. How old are you now?'

'Eleven and three-quarters,' said Luke.

'Aye, you're getting on a bit. Does thy father know you're over here?'

'Father won't mind. He likes us to mix with people. Sir, I'd like to invite your daughter to the fair.'

John grinned. 'My daughter, eh? Well, now, let's see. I have to be careful about her gentleman friends, but I can tell by your face it's serious. Go on then. Make sure you look after our Emma.'

She couldn't believe it. A visit to the fair? She thanked John, with a hug that took him by surprise, and skipped up the slope with Luke striding alongside. She thought how comfortable John had been talking to him, and maybe she ought to be the same. He couldn't help being a stuck-up posh boy.

'John's not my dad,' she said.

'Oh, sorry,' said Luke. 'I'm always putting my foot in it. Who is your dad?'

'I'm an orphan.' She checked herself. 'Well, that's what people say, but I don't believe my parents are dead.'

'Oh,' said Luke, who looked more confused than ever.

'I live with the Peaseleys. John's my foster brother. Where do you live?'

'Byrom Hall, just north of town. It's got ten bedrooms, three living rooms, and two water closets. Oh, and the park and gardens are good for exploring and hiding from Old Battleaxe.'

Emma was shocked by the gulf between them. 'A bit different from where I live,' she said. 'Two up, two down, and an ashpit privy.'

'How many servants have you got?' said Luke.

'Servants? That's a laugh. I'm the only servant. How many have you got?'

'Twelve,' said Luke.

'Twelve? That's an army!'

'They're all my friends, apart from Old Battleaxe.'

Along the promenade, the skyline was dominated by the Big Wheel, an awesome sight to Emma. They reached the outskirts of the fair and Luke pointed to a merry-go-round of brightly painted horses, with a steam organ playing oompah music.

'Shall we go on the Galloper?' he said.

They grabbed a horse each and Emma laughed excitedly as the world spun around her. Next they tried the swing-boats and Luke pulled so hard on the red and white rope, they nearly did a full orbit in the air. Emma just whooped with delight.

'You're pretty good,' said Luke. 'My brother Herbert would be screaming to get off by now.'

Further on, they found some side-shows, where huge queues were waiting to see the Lobster Lady, the Insect Man, and Old Boney the Living Skeleton.

'Do you want to see a freak?' said Luke. 'Lobster Lady's supposed to be the best. She's got claws instead of hands.'

'Ugh!' said Emma.

'If you like, we'll come back later, when the queues are shorter. What about the Big Wheel? Scared?'

'Course not,' said Emma, although she wasn't too sure.

'It's new this year. I've only been on it once and Herbert was sick all over me.'

This didn't do much for Emma's confidence. As they approached the Big Wheel, she heard the screams of people high in the sky and the butterflies started up in her stomach. An empty seat swung down and they climbed on board.

The wheel lurched upwards. Emma held on tight, and before long they were at the top, with a panorama of the sea that stretched for miles. She could see tiny figures moving around the beach, even the line of donkeys, and she faintly heard the singing of the minstrels.

Luke started to swing the seat violently back and fore. He looked at her, expecting her to scream, but she just flung her head back and breathed the fresh salt air. She wasn't scared any more. How could she be? She'd flown much higher than this, when she was a swan.

They returned to the ground, and saw the caravan of a fortune-teller, Gypsy Minerva Jones. Luke said it might be fun to go in, and soon Emma was sitting at a table, facing a bright crystal ball.

Gypsy Minerva, a wrinkled lady with brightly patterned head scarf, held out her hand.

'Cross my palm with silver,' she said, 'and I don't mean a Hardshaws' badge.'

Luke dug into his pocket and produced a silver sixpence. Emma was looking into the shining crystal, mesmerised. She could see water swirling round, gigantic waves, and a ship appearing, like the one in the Great Casting Hall. The sea went calm as the ship pulled into a beautiful harbour fringed with waving palms and huge ferns. On the deck, a pretty woman waved and smiled at her.

'Dear Emma,' she said. 'It's your mother. We've reached the Pacific Ocean.'

She tried to look closer at her mother's face, to see who it really was, but the sun was dazzling her......

'Emma, are you all right?' said Luke. 'The gypsy's telling your fortune.'

'You will rise to a high position,' said Minerva.

'She already has,' said Luke. 'She's been on the Big Wheel.'

Minerva scowled and ordered him outside. She returned to the crystal ball. 'You will travel to a distant land.....'

Emma's gaze was drawn back into the bright glass. The crystal ball began to expand into an enormous sphere and enveloped her in its shining embrace. Lights dazzled her eyes and she stood on a kind of platform facing hundreds of people. Her mother was at her side and they were singing a duet, and their voices soared above the audience. When they finished, the applause was deafening.

Hanging above them, a glass chandelier began to descend in a cascade of light, and brought Emma zooming back to the crystal ball. Gypsy Minerva Jones was telling her she would marry a handsome guardsman.

Emma shook her head. 'Tell me where my father is,' she begged.

Minerva looked into the ball. 'I see nothing,' she said. 'Your father is not here.'

'That's not true!' said Emma. 'I can see more than you. I've just seen my mam in the crystal ball.'

'Don't you question me,' said Minerva. 'Who are you? Some gypsy orphan come to steal my trade? Get out!'

As Emma stumbled out of the caravan, she found Luke sitting on the steps and a little line of people waiting. Her heart sank when she saw who was at the front of the queue, staring at her with malicious eyes.

Chapter 5
Flamingo Woman

'It's scruffy little Gingernut!' said Madge. 'What are you doin' here? A waste o' time you having your fortune told. You've only got one future, and that's washing my bed linen! Get back to the beach and look after the bairns.'

Emma looked at Luke, who grinned nervously. Then she ran, as fast as she could, away from being called her nickname in front of him, away from the 'sister' whose servant she was, back along the stalls, dodging the queues for the freak shows, and only stopping for breath near an attraction called the 'Hall of Mirrors'.

The thought of all that glass pulled her inside. She found rows of strange twisted mirrors which distorted her into grotesque shapes. Sometimes she was small and fat, with a blubbery mouth, then long and thin with arms touching the floor. One mirror gave her legs like stilts, a round body, and a long curly neck, all pink. Fascinated, she stood for a long time in front of it.

When she walked away, to her horror she found she really did have legs like stilts, and a pink curly neck, stretching upwards and making her eight feet tall. She looked in another mirror, a fat small one, but it didn't make any difference. In despair, she tottered out of the Hall of Mirrors and looked around.

A man shouted 'A freak! She's escaped!' and a woman screamed 'It's the Flamingo Woman!' and pulled her children to safety. Emma quivered with shock, all the way up her rubbery neck.

'What if I'm stuck like this for the rest of my life?' she thought. 'They'll put me in a freak show and Hannah Tunstall and Madge will pay to come and laugh at me. I'll never find my parents. They won't want me anyway, when I'm half a flamingo!'

With a moan, she bent her neck down as far as the ground, where she spotted a new penny. She picked it up in her long skinny fingers, and further on, a threepenny bit. Perhaps it might not be that bad after all. No-one could see what she could see. She curved her head round a corner and frightened the life out of the queue for the Lobster Lady. She lifted her neck above the gathering crowd, and felt like a powerful giant.

Emma decided to make the most of her new shape. Striding on spindly legs, she scattered the fairgoers, and reached Gypsy Minerva's caravan. Extending her long neck through the door, she stuck her tongue out, like a pink slimy snake, right into Madge's face, just as the gypsy was promising her a rich husband. Madge screamed, and knocked over the table and crystal ball.

With foul curses from Minerva in her ears, Emma dashed between two stalls, followed by a crowd of people shouting insults at her. When she turned round, she saw Luke in the middle of them, the last person she wanted to see her like this. She galloped off, with the crowd after her like a pack of hounds. She skirted a few more caravans, and came to the back of a sideshow, where a clown stood in front of a long mirror putting on his make-up.

When he saw the giant, elongated Emma, waving her pink neck, he yelled and ran off, as best he could in his baggy pants and flipper feet, falling over a few times in his panic. Emma stopped before the long mirror, an ordinary mirror at last, and concentrated hard.

As if by clockwork, her head descended, her feet came up, and there she was, her proper self again, the true Emma in the image of the glass, four foot nine inches tall, with freckles and flame-coloured hair.

She vanished into the crowd, and hurried from the fairground. Out of breath, she reached the beach, where John and Catherine asked her about the fair and she told them what she could. A little later, Luke appeared at the top of the steps and waved at her, but the governess appeared from nowhere, grabbed him by the ear and hauled him away.

George and Hetty, red-faced and tipsy, arrived just in time for dinner. Mr Hardshaw's caterers brought sandwiches and drinks, and the afternoon passed lazily as most people just sat or lay in the sand. George's snoring could be heard above all the others, although Hetty kept digging him in the ribs to stop.

Emma kept well away from the Hardshaws, and played with the children, making sandcastles and recovering from her glass fever. She regretted going with Luke now. He belonged to another class and was the boss's son, living in a mansion with a bevy of servants, far too grand for her. He would be master of Hardshaws one day, but she was lower than the lowest scullery maid.

About four o'clock, the army of glass workers and their families began to troop back to the station, where Madge was seen creeping out of the Ladies Waiting Room.

'I've been attacked by a monster freak,' she said. 'The pink Flamingo Woman. It was horrible and tried to eat me.'

'That's worse than seeing pink elephants,' said John. 'You'd best stay off the gin.'

When the train finally rumbled out of Sandhaven, the rolling motion sent the children off to sleep, and Emma soon followed them, dreaming she was the Flamingo Woman and chasing Miss Plews around the school yard.

She was brought violently awake as the whole carriage shook with a bang and the train juddered to a halt. The Peaseleys were thrown on top of each other, the children began to cry, and Emma hugged them tight, although terrified herself. She could hear people screaming and calling out frantically to each other.

John pulled down a window to look down the line. 'Summat's badly wrong. I can see clouds o' smoke, up ahead.'

The guard came down the track, shouting for everyone to stay in their carriages. The glassworkers shouted back at him, but he took no notice.

For nearly an hour they were stuck there, and nerves turned raw under the tension. Emma and Catherine tried to keep the children happy by playing games and singing songs. Hetty said she was having palpitations and needed a doctor, but George pulled out a small bottle of brandy, which proved a miracle cure. Madge was jabbering away, terrified it might be the Flamingo Woman coming to get her. It was turning into a proper madhouse, when the guard returned to make an announcement from the trackside.

'There's been a bomb on the line,' he said, 'and the first-class carriage has been knocked off the rails.'

'That'll be the Hardshaws,' said John.

Emma's heart sank, and she shouted through the window 'Was anybody killed?'

'Nay, lass,' said the guard, 'but the whole line's blocked and you'll have to walk home rest o' way.'

A chorus of groans filled the carriage, and the guard left in a hurry, before they caused him any grief. The Peaseleys lowered themselves onto the track and joined a column of people walking along the line towards a level crossing. At the gates, two policemen arrived on their penny farthings and ushered people off the railway and down a lane with the signpost 'Clayminster 7 miles.'

Hetty Peaseley was leaning heavily on George. 'I can't go on,' she moaned.

'What about me?' he said. 'It's like carrying a sack o' spuds.'

A pair of horses came rattling round the corner, pulling a four-wheeled coach, and stopped alongside a group of people whose clothes were blackened by soot and dirt, their faces scratched and their hats torn or missing.

'It's the Hardshaws,' said John. 'I didn't recognise them. Thank God they're all safe.'

Emma saw Luke standing with his mother. With his grey jacket ripped and his shoes missing, he looked more like the boys she normally met, bare-footed and grimy. She forgot he was the boss's son and hurried anxiously over to him.

His eyes lit up when he saw her. 'It's you!' he said. 'I thought you were my friend, but you ran off.'

Emma blushed, her usual bright red. 'I was upset,' she said.

'Who was that horrid woman?'

'She's a kind of older sister,' said Emma.

'Some sister,' said Luke. 'Hey, you missed the Flamingo Woman. Best freak I've ever seen. She was weird. All pink, with a long thin neck, and must have been ten feet tall.'

I'm getting bigger by the minute, thought Emma. Thank goodness he didn't recognise me. She quickly changed the subject.

'Where's Old Battleaxe?' she whispered.

'She's staying overnight with friends in Sandhaven. Pity she didn't get knocked around a bit, like the rest of us.

'Luke, get into the carriage at once,' said his mother.

'Mother, can Emma come too?'

Mrs Hardshaw looked down her nose at Emma.

'There's no room,' she said. 'No room at all. We must get home quickly and into a hot bath.'

Mr Hardshaw, who'd just finished talking to the policemen, joined his family and climbed into the coach, his face all tense and drawn. When the driver wheeled the horses round and rattled off in a cloud of dust, the crowd began to boo and shake their fists.

'So much for the Hardshaws,' said George. 'They'll be home in half-an-hour and it'll take us four or five.'

The long crocodile of people meandered along the country lane, and to add to their misery, the sky clouded over and raindrops spattered their faces. On John's back, Becky was crying and coughing, and little William couldn't go far without a rest. From a hill half-way to Clayminster, a weary Emma looked back and saw a plume of smoke rising from the train as it lay across the rails.

At the village of Fordhill, three miles from town, the public house was open and the glassworkers drank it dry. Some couldn't go any further and gained lodging for the night, including George and Hetty, who staggered upstairs. Madge met a local lad, a young farm labourer who was overwhelmed by the brassy town girl and unwisely spent his money on brandy and gin.

John decided the rest of them were better off at home. They managed to carry on walking, but it was two hours before the familiar stench of Clayminster reached their nostrils, wafting from the 'Stinky Brook', an open stream of untreated sewerage. Darkness was falling as they entered the streets, and the lamplighter was lighting the gas lamps, high on his ladder.

In the yellow glow, Emma could see a crowd of men outside the Bottle Works, another Hardshaw factory. Amidst the shouts and cheers, one voice rose clearly above the others, the voice of Alfred Peaseley chanting 'Up the Workers' Revolutionary Union!'

Alfred saw them and came across. Looking older than his twenty-four years, he shared John's sturdy build, but had a strange wild look in his eyes, unlike the calm good humour of his brother.

'Are you joining us, Johnny? We're goin' on strike.'

'Why should I join thee?' said John. 'I've got a good job at Hardshaws, haven't I?'

'You won't have for long,' said Alfred. 'What's happening here will happen to thee, sure as like. Mr Hardshaw's bringing in foreign glass blowers, from Belgium, and he's ordered some machines as well. Foot-operated bottlemaking machines. There'll be no work for Clayminster people, what with bottle-blowing Belgians and bottlemaking machines.' He grabbed John by the collar. 'You'd better join us, little brother, or else you'll never work at Hardshaws again.'

John pushed him aside. 'There aren't any Belgians,' he said. 'I don't know who's been spreading the rumour.'

'I saw some Belgians in the pub t'other night,' said Alfred. 'They'll take lower wages than us. Them Hardshaws are greedy.'

'Mr Hardshaw was nearly killed just now,' said John, 'on the train back from Sandhaven. Someone placed a bomb on the line. If he goes, you won't get a better boss.'

Alfred came straight back at him. 'Aye, and I've just heard he came home in his carriage, while the rest of you had to walk seven miles. That's just like him, look at his record as a magistrate, sending people to prison left right and centre, and all working people. No wonder someone tried to bomb him.'

The bottlemakers began to argue about the behaviour of Mr Hardshaw. Emma felt like telling them how kind he really was. Then someone shouted that the police were coming.

'Right, lads,' said Alfred. 'We can't have the bobbies interfering. Special meeting in *The Pickled Egg*. First round of drinks on me.'

A great cheer burst from the crowd and they all moved off towards the pub.

'Where's he getting all his money from?' said John. 'He's only on fifteen bob a week as a labourer.'

'Why didn't he come on the works trip?' said Emma.

'He's up to no good,' said John. 'He always were a rum lad, and now he's turned nasty. Come on, we'd best get home.'

Chapter 6
Welsh Chapel

The house was quiet, with no George or Hetty, and Emma soon had the children asleep while John took Catherine home. To the light of a solitary candle, Emma was doing her last chore of the day, which was to clean out the grate, when Madge burst in, smelling strongly of drink. She grabbed Emma by the hair and tweaked her nose till she yelped in pain.

'Here,' she said. 'Take this note to number 13. It's for the Jones brothers. I want a reply straightaway.'

She thrust the note into Emma's hand and pushed her out into the street. Tired out by the day's events, Emma nearly tore up the envelope, but dried her eyes on her pinafore and walked the four doors down to the Joneses.

Mr Jones opened the door, an elderly man nearing retirement as a copper smelter. Surprised, he brought Emma inside, where the rest of the family were sat round a table reading from the bible, his wife and their five grown-up sons, all unmarried.

'Welcome, Emma dear,' said Mrs Jones. 'We're just reading from St Paul's second epistle to Timothy. Go on, finish off, Lewis.'

'*Not given to wine, no striker, not greedy of filthy lucre, but patient, not a brawler, not covetous...*'

Lewis read in a passionate Welsh voice, and Emma felt her hand sweaty around the note from Madge, who seemed the complete opposite of St Paul's description.

'We started our bible-reading in Anglesey,' said Mrs Jones, 'and we've carried it on ever since. Did you know we have a Welsh chapel in town? You must come to our Sunday service to-morrow. We don't have a minister, but take it in turns. The boys are very good speakers on the sins of the flesh.'

The Jones brothers nodded, although the youngest one, Robert, was not very convincing. Emma handed over the note and Mrs Jones read it aloud.

Young lady of marriageable age, hard-working, respectable, well-spoken and shy, wishes to meet generous gentleman of means with a view to serious entanglement. Apply Madge Peaseley, number 9, Clarence Street.

'Serious entanglement?' cried Mr Jones. 'We'll have no such words spoken here. Your sister should be ashamed of herself.'

'She's not really my sister,' said Emma.

'We'd better say a prayer quickly,' said Mrs Jones.

The family mumbled a prayer in Welsh, while Mr Jones threw the note into the corner. Emma saw Robert open one eye and sneakily reach down and pocket the paper. The prayer stopped and Mrs Jones gave a sigh.

'My boys are all hard-working smelters at the

copper factory and have no time for scarlet women. Tell your sister they will only marry chapel-going girls of respectable nature, who can speak Welsh. Fancy sending you on errands at this time of night. Robert, see that Emma gets home safely.'

Robert leapt to his feet, put on his cap, and followed Emma out. He escorted along the street, and whispered in her ear.

'I don't mind seeing the young lady. I'm the youngest, see, and I was born here. The others keep going on about Anglesey, but it's all foreign to me. Tell your sister I'll reply to her note.'

He looked around guiltily and doffed his cap, before retreating down Clarence Street. At number 9, Madge grabbed hold of Emma and pulled her into the kitchen.

'Well? What did they say?' said Madge.

'You'll have to learn Welsh and go to chapel.'

Madge picked up the fire-irons and waved them at Emma. 'Is that it?'

'Well, one of them, Robert, said he might reply.'

'He's the youngest,' said Madge. 'He won't be earning much. Still, beggars can't be choosers.'

She went upstairs, all the time muttering to herself and soon there was silence as she fell into a drunken sleep. Emma found her lying on top of the bed, still in her day clothes, and crept exhausted onto her own ragged mattress in the corner. She heard John come in, the creak of his footsteps on the stairs, and wanted to talk to him, tell him about the crystal ball and her adventure in the Hall of Mirrors, but she was frightened he would think she was going mad.

Sleep came fitfully and the image of the crashed train kept recurring, till she sat bolt upright in bed, thinking another crash had happened. Then she recognised the raucous sound of a cornet and someone shouting, and remembered what day it was.

John, a member of the Clayminster Brass Band, was practising early for a Sunday march, and Madge was screaming down the stairs for him to stop. The bairns clambered over Emma, and another day of chores began, or so she thought.

At half-past nine there was a knock on the front door, and she found the Jones family standing there, Mr and Mrs Jones in front, and the five boys lined up behind them, all in their Sunday best, dark suits for the men and a long-sleeved navy blue dress for Mrs Jones, who also wore a hat with an ostrich feather.

'We thought you'd like to come to chapel with us,' said Mrs Jones.

'I haven't any best clothes,' said Emma, conscious of her threadbare pinafore and worn-out boots.

'That doesn't matter in the sight of the Lord,' said Mr Jones.

'Mr and Mrs Peaseley aren't home yet. I've got jobs to do.'

'It's all right, Emma,' said John, from behind her. 'You go to chapel. The children will be fine here. Madge will look after 'em, won't you, Madge?'

His sister was leaning out of the bedroom window,

disturbed by the knocking on the door. When she heard John's words, she turned puce with rage but managed to control herself and said sweetly 'Why, of course, dear brother. You know I always adore looking after the children. I can always go to chapel this evening.'

Emma could hardly believe her ears. Madge never lifted a finger to help the children and usually stayed in bed all Sunday. Then she saw the reason for the charade. Robert Jones, unseen by his parents, was merrily waving at Madge. When Mr Jones turned round, he instantly put his hands behind his back and assumed an innocent expression.

The family set off for chapel in single file, all carrying bibles, Mrs Jones at the front with Emma, Mr Jones at the back, keeping an eye on Robert.

The sun was shining more brightly to-day, and almost conquering the factory fumes. Along Victoria Road, Emma saw her friend Mary Meaney pushing a rusty old pram, with some other children, all bare-footed.

'Where're you goin'?' shouted Mary.

'To the Welsh chapel,' said Emma.

'They'll kidnap you and take you to Wales.'

'It'll be a change from Clarence Street.'

'Come wi' us, we're goin' to the Mucky Mountains.'

These were slag heaps on the edge of town, a favourite hunting ground for bits of free coal, but Mrs Jones ushered Emma round a corner, and across various streets, until they reached a long brick-built building with an arched doorway.

Inside, every head turned when the Joneses entered and took their places in a pew near the front. The chapel was full, and a small organ accompanied the hymn singing, all in Welsh and completely beyond Emma's understanding.

She gazed around the small crowded building, which had two rectangular windows down the side, in plain glass, and her heart jumped as she saw a handsome man with wavy copper-coloured hair looking through one, and a woman's face through the other, a pretty smiling face, like she'd seen in the crystal ball, but wearing a white bonnet.

'Don't stare at the windows,' said Mrs Jones. 'It's hymn number ninety three.'

Emma looked at her, then back at the windows. The faces had gone.

'But I don't know any Welsh.'

'I'll translate,' said Mrs Jones, and she whispered in Emma's ear before each verse of the hymn. Then Lewis Jones went forward to the pulpit and delivered a passionate sermon, not a word of which Emma could understand, without Mrs Jones's help.

'It's about demon drink,' she said. 'After chapel, there's a meeting of the Temperance Movement in the Town Hall, for people to sign the pledge.'

When the service ended and people moved outside, Emma glanced at the windows, in case a man and a woman were really looking in. Nobody was around, not a soul in sight. Was it glass teasing her again? Why couldn't it show her real people? She felt lonely and abandoned, even in the middle of the noisy Welsh crowd which assembled on the pavement.

Down the road came the sound of a brass band, and Emma watched it swing round the corner and past the chapel. Among the cornet players, John was marching along proudly, and further back PC Fossett was playing a huge euphonium which twisted around his neck and nearly swallowed him up. Behind the band came the various groups from different churches and chapels, all carrying their banners in support of the Temperance Movement. The Welsh contingent tagged onto the rear, which meant Emma had to march too.

'Alcohol is killing this town,' said Mrs Jones. 'We have a hundred and sixty two public houses and the police courts are full of drunks. Some are so bad they have to be taken to court in a wheelbarrow.'

'Some of them fall in the canal,' said Mr Jones.

'Last week, one fell on the railway line and was run over,' said Mrs Jones. 'Let it be a warning to all you young people.' She gave a stern look in Robert's direction, as one who might most be tempted.

Emma felt out of place, marching in her everyday clothes. She hoped no-one would see her, but when they stopped by St Mary's Parish Church, to collect another group, she heard a shout of 'Emma!' and saw Luke Hardshaw on the pavement, watching with his family. He ran across and grinned at her.

'What are you doing here? I didn't know you were Welsh.'

'These are my neighbours,' she whispered. 'Don't make a scene.'

'I'm going to march with you,' he said.

A harsh voice interrupted them, making Emma back away in alarm.

'Luke, you ill-mannered boy, come here this instant!'

Chapter 7

Glass Goblet

Striding towards them came the stern woman in black, Madame Renoir, the vulture-like governess. When she saw Emma, her eyes narrowed into slits and her pointed nose wrinkled in disgust. She spoke in a foreign accent, unlike any Clayminster sound.

'Who is this guttersnipe?' she said.

'She's not a guttersnipe,' said Luke. 'She's my friend.'

'Don't be impertinent. You cannot make friends with urchins like her. You have certain standards to keep up. Come away from that wretched girl.'

Madame Renoir grabbed him by the arm and pulled him back on the pavement. The band struck up *Onward Christian Soldiers*, and Emma was swept along with the marchers. She wanted to stay with Luke, but knew they were worlds apart, separated by class, by money, and by Old Battleaxe.

When she looked back at the church, she saw Mr and Mrs Hardshaw, young Herbert, and the nanny with the two toddlers, all spruce and clean in their Sunday clothes. Mr Hardshaw was helping his wife into a fine two-horse carriage. The governess dragged Luke along to join them.

Emma wished she could ride in the carriage down

Clarence Street. That would show Hannah and Madge a thing or two. She'd wave at them like Queen Victoria and leave them goggle-eyed. What if Luke asked her to dinner with his family? She was bound to make a fool of herself, and the governess would be horrible about her table manners. On the other hand, Luke would be good fun, and she'd be curious to see his home.

She shook herself out of her daydream. All those silly thoughts were a waste of time. A ragged little servant girl like her, she'd never get an invitation to Byrom Hall, not in a month of Sundays.

When the procession reached the Town Hall, people began to queue under the ornate porch, ready to sign the pledge never to drink again. Emma saw Mrs Hardshaw and the governess join the queue, but Mr Hardshaw loudly declared he wouldn't surrender his daily glass of brandy. He went to talk to some of his workers.

Emma edged closer to the carriage and listened. The nanny was singing nursery rhymes to the toddlers. She had a soft, melodious voice and Emma nearly joined in.

'Sarah, why don't you go into Music Hall?' said Luke.

'I might, one day,' said the nanny.

'You'll be good,' said Luke. 'I'll come and watch you, and sit in the three shilling sofa seats.'

The nanny laughed. 'Oh yes, and after the show, you can buy me caviar and champagne!'

'That's naughty,' said Herbert, sounding prim and proper.

Mrs Hardshaw returned to the carriage, full of enthusiasm for what had been said about the evils of drink. She had a crystal goblet in her hand and called Mr Hardshaw over.

'Freddie, look, the Temperance Movement have presented me with a glass. It's inscribed in Latin around the rim – *Solum Aqua,* which means 'only water'.'

Mr Hardshaw took the goblet by the stem and eyed it disdainfully. 'Give me a brandy glass any time.'

His wife pursed her lips and climbed into the carriage. The governess returned and the coachman prepared to leave. Emma's mind was in a turmoil. After listening to Luke and the nanny, she wanted to go with them even more. She ran to Mrs Jones and told her she would have to go home.

When she arrived back at the carriage, Mr Hardshaw was holding the goblet up to the sun and examining the texture.

'Cheap Belgian crystal,' he said.

His wife leant out of the carriage door. 'Don't be tiresome, Freddie. Pass it to me.'

Now was Emma's only chance to see Byrom Hall, and answer a nagging question in her mind. She hesitated, remembering her scare with the lemonade bottle, but just as Mr Hardshaw was passing the goblet to his wife, a shaft of sunlight made it sparkle, and Emma seized her opportunity.

Catching the sun's ray, she flashed into the goblet and moulded herself to its shape. Mrs Hardshaw blinked, and placed her on the leather seat. Emma could see and hear clearly through her crystal body, but as the carriage lurched into motion, she started to roll and Herbert looked at her with an evil eye, as if ready to crush her.

What had she done now? Here she was, stripped of her clothes, engraved with letters, stuck on one leg, and about to be smashed by the murderous Herbert. To her relief, Mrs Hardshaw took her on her lap, and the boy scowled in frustration.

Leaving the cobbled streets of Clayminster, the horses gathered speed into the countryside. Emma's daydream of visiting Byrom Hall was coming true, although not how she imagined it. She listened anxiously to the Hardshaws chatting away. The nanny seemed like part of the family, but the governess kept herself aloof.

A mile or two outside town they turned into a long pebbled drive. Through an avenue of trees, the carriage approached a large sandstone house, with many windows and a cluster of tall chimneys. Reflected in her crystal glass, Emma thought it grand enough to be a royal palace. On a vivid green lawn facing the front porch, a fountain of water sprayed upwards in glittering silver drops. The horses came to a halt outside a porch of white columns.

'Luke, be a good boy and take this goblet down to Annie,' said Mrs Hardshaw. 'Tell her to clean it and place it in the dining room.'

Clutching Emma in his hand, Luke jumped from the carriage and ran towards the big panelled front door, which opened as if by magic. A housemaid stood back to let him through.

'Luke, be careful you reckless boy!' cried Mrs Hardshaw.

He hurried through the hall and down some stairs, giving Emma the fright of her life, as she fully expected to drop from his hand and smash on the floor. He reached the kitchen, a hive of activity, with steam rising from pans on a black stove and a red-faced chubby woman stirring a basin. Two maids were helping prepare the meal and another glided up and down the stairs with cutlery.

'Annie, here's a glass for you. Mother says clean it and have it put in the dining room.

The cook greeted him with a warm smile. 'What's this then?'

'Oh, they gave it to mother for signing the pledge.'

Emma recognised the cook as Annie Jones, the sole daughter of the Joneses, who'd escaped the chapel life for that of the kitchen. On her days off, she often came down to Clarence Street to visit her family.

Annie took the goblet and placed it on the table. Emma had a good view all round, but was beginning to steam up a little. The cook gave a big sigh, and presented Luke with a large strawberry. Her soft brown eyes examined him.

'Growing up fast, eh? I remember when you were a baby in a pram. Noisy little beggar! What have you been up to to-day?'

'Oh, same old church, but we saw a procession, and Emma was there, remember, the girl I told you about.'

'Ah yes, Emma Peaseley. Lives near my mam and

dad. Poor lass. She was in the workhouse till she was nine, then the Peaseleys took her in. Out of the frying pan and into the fire, if you ask me.'

'She's got red hair,' said Luke.

'It's nice hair,' said Annie.

'I didn't say it wasn't,' said Luke, and for the first time Emma saw him blush.

'There's nothing wrong with red hair,' said Annie. 'Your Uncle James had red hair, all wavy like, and a fine moustache, very dashing he was in his colonel's uniform, when he was in the Volunteers. All the young ladies fancied him.'

'Emma doesn't look a bit like him,' said Luke. 'I've seen his picture.'

'Well, she wouldn't look like him, would she, not unless you put her in a uniform.'

A gong sounded upstairs, a relief to Emma, who'd heard enough about the colour of her hair.

'I'll murder that butler,' said Annie. 'I haven't even mixed the gravy yet. You'd better run upstairs!'

A housemaid took Emma to the sink and washed her in warm water, which was pleasant and soothing, like having your own servant to give you a bath. She was dried in a clean tea-towel and carried upstairs. Life as a glass goblet did not seem so bad, when you were being treated like an important person. A dark-suited butler placed her carefully on the sideboard, with the motto *Solum Aqua* in full view.

Emma looked around her, an easy task when your body was a complete circle. She nearly wobbled over at the sight.

Chapter 8
Walking a Tightrope

All the rooms of number 9, Clarence Street, could have fitted into the dining room of Byrom Hall. She stared at the rich velvet curtains and mahogany sideboard, the decorated ceiling and the glass chandelier, the long table set for six people and the embossed silver cutlery.

The Hardshaws arrived. The toddlers were not present, but the nanny and governess were given places. The nanny had a pretty face and smiling eyes, whichever way Emma looked at her, but the governess stayed grim and forbidding.

On the table, Emma had never seen so much food. It took the combined efforts of the butler and two housemaids to serve it. First there was soup, something called asparagus, then venison, a kind of meat, with potatoes and cabbage and carrots and peas.

'Annie's done us proud again,' said Mr Hardshaw. 'How is she to-day? She looked out of sorts last week.'

'She never used to be like that,' said Mrs Hardshaw. 'It's only since she's been going out with Reginald the coachman. High as a kite one minute, and down in the dumps the next. She keeps waiting for Reginald to propose, but he never does.'

The governess eagerly threw in some gossip.

'They had a blazing row because he wouldn't take her on the works outing. He said he was playing in a cricket match, but someone saw him in a public house and told Annie.'

'Reginald ought to know better,' said Mrs Hardshaw.

The nanny spoke up. 'Ma'am, if I may say so, I think he loves her, but he's very independent. She says he only wants her for her cooking, but I've seen the look in his eye.'

'They get on fine,' said Luke. 'I saw them cuddling in the stables.'

'That's enough from you, young man,' said Mr Hardshaw. 'Concentrate on your studies, never mind what's going on in the stables. Your last school report was a disaster. Bottom in Latin and bottom in Greek, but worst of all bottom in mathematics.'

'Father, it's the teachers,' said Luke. 'They're boring.'

His mother intervened. 'You've had good teaching,' she said. 'First with Madame Renoir here, and now at one of the best public schools in the country. I want you to go to university and become prime minister, like Mr Gladstone.'

'Me, prime minister?' said Luke. 'Please, mother, I'd sooner run a fairground or travel the world in search of treasure.'

'Don't be absurd,' said Mrs Hardshaw. 'You're just like your Uncle James, full of wild notions.'

'He's dead,' said Herbert.

'Yes, we know, dear,' she said.

'Nothing wrong with my brother James,' said Mr Hardshaw. 'It's taken me ten years to work out a plan for a non-stop glass furnace, but he'd have done it in five minutes. A genius with glass, everybody said so. I rue the day I ever sent him to that glassworks in Belgium. Murdered, in cold blood he was, and the numb-skull police still haven't found out who did it.'

'Come, come, Freddy dear,' said Mrs Hardshaw. 'Not in front of the children'

'Yes, but who's going to run the glassworks, when I pop my clogs? said Mr Hardshaw.

'I can't be prime minister and run a glassworks,' said Luke.

'Eat your cabbage and have less to say,' said his mother.

'Children should be seen and not heard,' said Madame Renoir.

The company went silent, as they absorbed this ponderous comment. Emma felt sorry for Luke and wanted to take his side. Why couldn't he go in search of treasure?

Mrs Hardshaw changed the subject. 'Have the police found anything yet about the railway bomb?'

'No, but there are mad people about,' said Mr Hardshaw, 'jealous, angry people, who hate the rule of law and the rights of property owners. Only this year, the Tsar of Russia was killed by a dynamite bomb and a couple of weeks ago, the President of the United States was shot with a pistol.'

'You're only a glassmaker dear,' said Mrs Hardshaw, 'not a king or a president.'

'Aye, but I want to be king of glassmaking,' insisted Mr Hardshaw, 'and someone's out to stop me. Look at that bottlemakers' strike. A foul rumour it was, about the Belgians. I wouldn't hire any foreigners, not above our Clayminster lads. It's true I want bottlemaking machines, but we have to modernise, or we're finished. Now this new workers' union has made me postpone the plan. It's a conspiracy against Hardshaws, and there's dirty work afoot.'

Emma listened, and remembered Alfred's little scene outside the Bottle Works. Was he leading a conspiracy against the Hardshaws?

'Don't get worked up, Freddy,' said Mrs Hardshaw. 'Look, it's your favourite dessert.'

Strawberries and cream arrived on the table and when they were dished out, Herbert complained that Luke had a bigger helping than he did. Madame Renoir gave him a few strawberries from Luke's plate, but Luke was too quick and stole some back from the governess when she wasn't looking. She turned and examined her plate, counted her strawberries and glowered at Luke, but he'd already eaten the evidence.

Emma saw the nanny giggling and started to laugh herself, which came out as a tinkling sound. When Mrs Hardshaw looked up, she tried desperately to stop her glass shaking.

'There's my sober goblet,' said Mrs Hardshaw. '*Solum Aqua*, that's what it says. Read that, Luke, and obey. I don't want you turning into a drunkard. There's no room for drunkards in this house.'

Mr Hardshaw's strawberry went down the wrong way, and he coughed for several minutes.

'Sarah, I think it's time for the children to go and play outside,' said Mrs Hardshaw.

The nanny led the two boys into the gardens. Emma wanted to follow them and explore the place. She waited patiently while the dinner was finished. Mrs Hardshaw retired for a rest, while her husband went for a smoke and a sly brandy in his study.

Before long, all the dishes had been cleared and the dining room was deserted. Quietness ruled in the house. On the dining-room sideboard, the crystal goblet flickered in a ray of sunlight and began to wobble on its stem.

Suddenly it toppled over and poured out its contents. Not wine, not even water, but a girl with red-gold hair and a scared look in her eyes. Emma straightened her clothes, put the goblet back in its place, and slipped through the French windows into the garden.

Outside her glass disguise, she felt conspicuous, but glad to be on two legs and walking again. Across the lawn, she could see a path through some silver birches. She scurried over, and at the bottom of a young tree, saw a bronze plaque with some wild flowers placed around it. She read the inscription:

Planted in Loving Memory of James Albert Hardshaw 1839–1870.

'Emma, what are you doing here?'

She nearly jumped out of her skin. It was Luke, staring wide-eyed at her.

'I wanted to see where you lived,' she said, her face a bright red.

'How on earth did you get here?'

'Oh, I er – got a lift on a coal cart.'

'You're incredible. I've never known a girl like you.'

'Don't let them catch me.'

'Everyone's having a rest, the servants as well. It's always the same on Sunday.'

'What about the nanny?'

'Sarah Danby? She's had to take Herbert for a change of clothes. He had an accident. I was pretending to show him the hole where the rabbit went in *Alice's Adventures in Wonderland* and he fell over on some rabbit droppings. Accidentally, of course. Pity about his sailor suit.'

Emma smiled. 'I thought the nanny had bairns to look after.'

'She has an under-nurse to help. So, you've found Uncle James's tree, have you? Someone keeps putting the flowers there, but we don't know who it is. Come on, I'll show you some of the house. I've a secret way in.'

She didn't like to tell him she'd already seen the kitchen and dining room. Dodging between trees, he led her through a side entrance, creeping up the back stairs and onto a long landing. The first door was wide open and Emma could see a floor scattered with toys.

'Have a good look,' said Luke, 'before Herbert

comes and finds us.'

Emma hadn't seen toys like them, never in her life, dolls with fine dresses, and dolls' houses with tiny furniture, huge model trains on a track all around the room, two rocking horses, toy soldiers in red uniforms lined up for battle against half-naked Zulus, and a tiny stage for a puppet show.

Luke went to a table and showed her a rectangular box with two glass eye-pieces in the front.

'This is my favourite,' he said. 'The stereoscope! All you need is a photo-card.'

From a pile of cards on the table, he showed one to Emma. On it were two photographs side by side, of a man on a tightrope, with a balancing pole, high above a swirling river.

'That's Blondin,' said Luke. 'He's the world's greatest tightrope walker and that's him crossing the rapids at Niagara Falls. He's did it once with a stove on his back, and stopped in the middle to fry himself an egg.'

Emma laughed, but he insisted it was true. 'Why two pictures?' she said. 'They look the same.'

He slid the card into the back of the stereoscope. 'See what happens,' he said, 'when you look through the lenses. Go on, put your eyes to the glass.'

Emma paused, knowing it was risky for her to go near glass, but couldn't stop herself. She bent down to the box and looked in. At first, each of her eyes saw a separate picture, but then the photographs merged into one, making objects stand out like they were real. The man on the tightrope stood so lifelike, she felt she could reach out and pick up the tiny figure. Down below him the torrent foamed and people were watching from the sides of the river. A gigantic waterfall cascaded nearby.

Now she began to hear the roar of water, growing louder, and the spray from the waterfall began to glitter like diamonds.

In a splash of light, the glass lenses pulled her into the picture, and to her horror she found herself holding onto the rope-walker's back and being carried through the cool air, miles above the river. Misty drops sprinkled her face from the crashing falls.

The man stepped along the tightrope as if nothing had happened. He swayed from side to side, using his pole to balance, and the taut rope quivered beneath them She clung on for dear life, trying not to look into the dizzy depths, then noticed his hair was copper-red like hers. She cried out.

'Dad, is that you?'

'Hush, Emma,' said the man. 'Wait till we've reached the other side. You're a ton weight!'

He knew her name. It must be her dad!

But they never reached the other side. There was a sudden crack, and he wavered dangerously, making her slide from his back. She grabbed hold of the rope as he plunged downwards with a terrible cry, towards the rocks below. Swinging in mid-air, she shouted desperately for her father, but she couldn't hold on, the rope slipped from her grasp and she was falling......

Chapter 9

The Bacchus Vase

Before she hit the rocks, the picture broke up into two images again, and she tumbled backwards onto the floor of the nursery, trembling with fright.

'Emma, what's the matter?' said Luke. 'You were shouting dad or something.'

'My dad – ' said Emma, then quickly stopped herself. 'I felt dizzy, like I was falling into the river.'

'Grand view, isn't it? Just like real.'

'Yes,' she said. 'Just like real.'

She rubbed her eyes and tried to think clearly. Why did her father drop, when he seemed so secure-footed? What was the crack? A rifle shot, like she'd sometimes heard when the Volunteers practised in the fields?

'Who did you say was on the tightrope?' she asked.

'Blondin. He's French.'

'Oh. Did he ever fall off the rope?'

'No, he's still alive and performing at the Crystal Palace. He carried his daughter across once, but they stopped him doing it, so he pushed a lion across in a wheelbarrow. Are you all right now?'

She nodded, but was still shaking from what she'd witnessed.

Luke wound up a clockwork train and let it run down the track. 'Father says we'll have electric lights and electric trams by the end of the century. He wants to build a generator in the garden, using the old water mill. He's mad about machines and new-fangled devices.'

'He's nice, your father,' said Emma.

'Well, he's all right. He's only flogged me a few times.'

'What for?'

'Well, once I put a frog in Old Battleaxe's handbag. Then I put some tadpoles in the thunder box.'

'What's a thunder box?'

'Come and see!'

He led her out onto the landing and past some bedrooms to a door at the end, marked 'Lavatory'. Proudly, he pushed the door open, making a fanfare with his voice. At seat level, Emma saw a white porcelain bowl, decorated with a blue flower pattern and the inscription 'Thunder Box'. A chain hung from a cistern above, and when Luke pulled the handle, water cascaded into the bowl, making Emma step back in surprise.

'It's one of father's better ideas,' said Luke. 'Would you like a go on it?'

'What?' said Emma, her face turning bright red.

'Oh well, at least you know where it is.'

Walking back across the landing, Luke pushed open a bedroom door. It was a large room with a wardrobes and a washstand and a fair-sized bed in the middle.

'This is my bedroom,' he said.

Emma's eyes widened in surprise. 'A bed with a room all to itself?'

Luke laughed and showed the view from the window, which overlooked a lawn and shrubbery. 'Sometimes I shin down the drainpipe,' he said, 'if I'm gated in my room. Come on, I'll show you the library.'

He led the way down the main stairs, like they were two cat-burglars, and came to a pair of double doors, which he pushed slowly open. Emma saw a spacious room with bookshelves high to the ceiling, and several glass-fronted cabinets containing glass vases and jugs and bowls of different colours.

'This is the library,' said Luke. 'See, all this Roman glass which Uncle James brought back from his travels.'

The colours of the Roman glass played in front of Emma's eyes, a large blue jug, rounded and sleek, a green vase decorated with patterns, a deep yellow bowl, another one of turquoise, and a glass fish sparkling in the light, with delicate scales and fins carved on it.

'Over here's the best one,' said Luke.

He moved to another cabinet, wholly occupied by a large bell-shaped vase, which was deep blue with white figures engraved upon it. A long-haired muscular youth was riding a chariot pulled by two tigers and over the chariot hung trails of vines and bunches of grapes.

'It's the Bacchus vase,' said Luke. 'That's him, the

god of wine. Doesn't he look good?'

The eyes on the god lit up and gazed at Emma. He beckoned and she felt herself floating into the cabinet, to join him on the chariot.

The tigers roared and pulled them along a paved road, with massive tombstones and statues on either side. Ahead she could see the glistening towers and rooftops of a great city, and crowds had gathered in front of a high gateway, some of them in white togas, others throwing flowers in their path. Bacchus turned and spoke.

'You want to find your mother?'

'Yes please,' said Emma, hardly able to speak.

'She's a slave to the emperor of Rome. But you can set her free.'

The gates of Rome opened to them, and the crowds parted as the chariot reached the emperor's palace. He came out on a balcony, in a long flowing toga of purple.

Emma gasped. It was Mr Hardshaw, looking very classical, his hair combed forward in true Roman style. By his side stood Mrs Hardshaw in a delicate silk dress, her blonde hair piled high in elaborate curls. She stared defiantly at Bacchus and turned her back on him, but when the tigers roared, she quickly faced the god of wine.

'Where is the slave woman who sings?' said Bacchus.

'I am here,' said a gentle voice, and a pretty, brown-haired woman with a bright smile stepped forward onto the balcony. She wore a simple white tunic, tied with a thin girdle, and Emma knew who it was, the moment she saw her.

'I have brought your daughter,' said Bacchus, 'who was lost in the wilderness.'

The slave woman held out her arms and Emma dashed eagerly up the steps to the balcony, where she was stopped by the emperor.

'Are you really her mother?' he said to his slave.

'Yes,' said the woman. 'Her father was killed in a far-off province.'

'Who did it?' said Emma. 'Who killed my father?'

'Get away!' shouted the emperor. 'You shouldn't be here!'

He tried to grab Emma, but Bacchus threw his vines around the emperor's neck and began to strangle him. Soldiers ran forward and hurled spears, but Bacchus brushed them aside like twigs. Emma could still hear the emperor shouting 'You shouldn't be here! You shouldn't be here!'

The chaotic scene faded into the blue glass, and she was back in the library, clutching hold of the cabinet. An angry Mr Hardshaw was pulling her away from the Bacchus vase.

'Get away! You shouldn't be here! You're trying to steal my vase, aren't you?' He looked more closely at her. 'I know you, you're the Peaseley girl. Who let you in? You little thief, you're in league with somebody.'

Luke came through the door. 'No, father, no. She came here to see me. I was showing her the glass, then something funny happened and she just vanished.'

'I've had enough of your cock and bull stories,'

said Mr Hardshaw. 'You'll get a thrashing for this. There's valuable stuff in here.'

'I knew she was trouble from the moment I saw her,' said a harsh voice. It was Madame Renoir, framed in the doorway like an avenging demon. 'That person will never rise from the gutter where she belongs.'

The nanny came in with Herbert, who said his brother had pushed him into some muck. Mr Hardshaw went another shade of purple.

'Sarah, why can't you control the children? That's your job, isn't it? Here, take this young woman home. I'll see her parents in the morning. She's lucky not to be spending the night in the lock-up.'

Emma was devastated. Called a thief, by Mr Hardshaw, whom she admired so much! As she left the house, the whole place seemed full of shouting and anger. Sarah asked where she lived, and ushered her into a carriage, which rumbled away from Byrom Hall and along the country lanes.

At first Emma sat crumpled and pensive, but unwound a little when Sarah asked how she met Luke. She told her about Sandhaven and the fair. Since the nanny seemed so warm and sympathetic, she told her more, about the Peaseleys, about school, and about her time in the workhouse. She said nothing about her glass fever, but when they reached the cobblestones of Clayminster, she had to speak out.

'Miss, have you had any children of your own?'

'Why do you ask?'

'Well, you seem so nice with children, and I just thought – '

Sarah's face clouded over. 'I had a baby once,' she said, 'but they took her away from me.'

'Why?'

'I was penniless and sick, and living in the workhouse. The fever left me with hallucinations and they thought I was insane and put me in the madhouse. They separated me from my baby, and by the time I recovered, she was dead.'

'Oh,' said Emma. 'It was a baby girl then?'

'Yes.'

'Your baby, how old would it be now?'.

'Eleven.'

'That's my age.' Emma paused, while she gathered more courage to speak out. 'I could be your baby, couldn't I? I was in the workhouse too.'

For a moment, Sarah looked thunderstruck, then she recovered and smiled. 'Emma, it's a nice thought, but I have to face up to reality. My baby died in a typhoid epidemic.'

'They said my mother died when I was born, but I've seen these visions.'

'What visions?

'You won't call me loony or a witch, will you?'

'No, of course not. Tell me.'

'Well, I can see things in glass and make things happen. I was looking at a glass vase just now, and a lady came to me, and it was my mother!'

'Now, now, don't go on so,' said Sarah. 'How did you know it was your mother?'

'They said it was, even Bacchus said it was!'

'Dear Emma, you've just been daydreaming.'

The horses slowed to a halt outside number 9, Clarence Street. The curtains shifted on the windows of neighbouring houses, as people watched the uncommon arrival, like a visit from royalty. Emma wanted to say more, now she'd told her secret, but Sarah began to help her down from the carriage.

'You think I'm mad, don't you?' said Emma. 'But the lady in the glass vase, it was you!'

'Emma, don't go on like this. I've told you, my baby died!'

Sarah had tears in her eyes now, making Emma feel even more wretched for upsetting her. The front door opened and George came out. The nanny had a quick word with him, before climbing back into the carriage. As the horses wheeled away, George pushed his foster-daughter through the door.

'Where've you been? Bothering the Hardshaws have you? There's loads o' jobs waiting for thee.'

Madge came bustling downstairs. 'What d'ye know, there's been a horse and carriage outside, all posh like.'

'It's the Hardshaws,' said George. 'Emma here, she's just been brought back.'

'Emma and the Hardshaws?' shouted Madge. 'They wouldn't come near a scruff like her. I always knew she was a little liar. Where the hell has she been? She's got the housework to do, and our dinner to cook. And what about the bairns? I'm not looking after them one minute more, the little brats.'

'Stop wittering,' said George. 'Them bairns have been with John at the park for the last hour. Now then,

Emma, what were you doin' at Hardshaws?'

Emma stood there, fighting back her tears and desperate to tell them some story or other, anything to shut them up. She was saved by the sudden arrival of Alfred, who blundered into the kitchen, red-faced and dishevelled.

'Look what the tide's brought in,' said George. 'Another troublemaker. Where've you been? Were you mixed up wi' all that bombing yesterday?'

Alfred was in no mood for questions. 'Are you talking to me or chewing a brick?'

'Speak to me like that again and I'll take my belt to thee.'

'Aye, you and whose army?'

George reached for his buckle, then hesitated. Alfred was bigger than he was and half his age. He tried another tactic.

'You're not my proper son and never will be.'

'Shut yer gob, you big fat bag o' lard!'

Alfred spat on the floor and went out by the back door, while George sank ashen-faced into a chair. From upstairs, Hetty shouted down that all the racket was disturbing her Sunday rest, and she was only just back from Sandhaven.

Emma went down the yard for some water. She sank to her knees near the tap, and at last began to cry, in hard, hurting sobs, unable to stop herself this time.

Chapter 10
Sixpenny Spectacles

All that night, the events of Sunday and her words with Sarah tumbled through Emma's fevered brain. When she awoke, the nightmares stayed with her, that she'd really lost her father, and couldn't prove Sarah was her mother, and faced prison for breaking into Byrom Hall.

Perhaps she'd told Sarah too much. The fear of being called a witch returned to haunt her. They would drag her off to a lonely hill and burn her at the stake, a slow and horrible death. It might be the only way to get rid of her glass fever, as when they burnt the cholera corpses. She buried her head in a pillow and struggled to shake off her terror.

Monday morning's chores brought her back to reality, the same old business of dressing and feeding the toddlers, preparing breakfast for the others, and making up the snaps. At least George seemed to have forgotten about the Hardshaws. Hetty stayed in bed, complaining of a sick headache, hot flushes, and a trembling sensation.

'I've had some terrible dreams,' she said, 'and I've found some blotches on my skin.'

'You'll have eaten summat bad,' said George. 'It's Emma's cooking. Take some of your medicine.'

'I've tried a new one,' said Hetty, 'Cockles Universal Purifying Mixture, but it's made me worse. I've got to see a doctor.'

'We can't afford a doctor,' said George. 'The workhouse has a matron.'

'You won't find me dead in a workhouse,' said Hetty. 'You can loosen your purse and pay for a doctor. Dr Hurst, in Commercial Street, he's my favourite.'

'What about the bairns?'

'Emma will have to miss school and look after them. I can't have another night like last night, what with you snoring as well.'

George grumbled like a rumbling volcano, but agreed to take her to the doctor's on his way to work. Emma often missed school because of Hetty's illnesses, but had a hard job convincing Miss Plews she wasn't playing truant.

When the Peaseleys left, Emma had jobs to do around the house, as well as looking after the children. Under a cushion in the sitting-room, she found Hetty's spectacles, bought for sixpence at the market. Hetty needed them to read the tiny newsprint of the *Clayminster Chronicle* and to keep up with her romantic serial, 'Mabel's Secret Love'.

Emma turned the spectacles round in her hand and pondered their use. Were they good glass or bad glass? Would they help her find her parents, or simply bring her more trouble? Could they correct her feverish vision? There was only one way to find out.

Her heart beat fast, as she clipped the wire ends

around her ears and peered through the lenses. The room seemed hazy, then suddenly cleared, and she could see through the wall into next door's house. She nearly tore the glasses off, but curiosity got the better of her.

There was Mary's dad, Mr Meaney, home from night shift at the colliery, washing himself in a tin bath while Mrs Meaney poured hot water over him. The coal dust streamed down his back in rivulets. He finished bathing and began to stand up. Emma turned quickly away.

Her gaze shot through several more brick walls until she met the parlour of the Joneses and found Mrs Jones intently reading the *Clayminster Chronicle*. Emma focused her eyes and smiled when she saw the headline 'Mabel's Secret Love.' Obviously a strict chapel life didn't stop Mrs Jones enjoying a romantic read, but when Robert came in, she quickly pushed the paper behind a cushion.

Emma stepped back, impressed by the power of the sixpenny spectacles. She wondered how far she could see in them, and ran upstairs to the front bedroom. Clarence Street was built on a slope, allowing her to see the rooftops of the other houses, but now she looked far beyond them, down Victoria Road, across the canal, cutting through the smoke and grime, past the Great Casting Hall and into the cornfields on the edge of town.

She swivelled round and brought her telescopic eyes onto the grim brickwork of Clayminster workhouse. A woman was walking to the entrance, a familiar figure, and now she was knocking on the door. Why was she calling? She look too well dressed to be an inmate.

Emma tried to concentrate on the woman's face, but down below the front door of the house shuddered to a thunderous knocking and the children began to cry. Zooming back to close-up vision, she scuttled downstairs, and used the spectacles to gaze through the wooden door and onto the street.

Two men stood on the pavement, in front of a horse and carriage.

There was no mistaking Mr Hardshaw in his top hat and whiskers, looking grim and determined, and PC Fossett, with his bristling beard and comical helmet. Obviously they intended to arrest her and throw her in the lock-up. She panicked, and gathering the children, ran through the kitchen and into the back yard.

She crouched with the little ones in a corner, telling them to be quiet, because it was just a little game of hide and seek. She prayed the two men would go away when no-one answered the door. Then she heard footsteps, and gazing with her spectacles through the back gate, saw PC Fossett coming down the alley.

Back into the house she scrambled, pulling the children with her. What could she do? She thought of running down to Mrs Jones and hiding there, or calling at the Meaneys, if Mr Meaney had finished his bath.

'It's our turn to go outside,' she told the children.

'Be very quiet.'

She crept with them into the hall and shot her gaze through the front door again. She could only see the horse and carriage, but behind her, she could hear PC Fossett opening the kitchen door. A pity George Peaseley wasn't there, to send him packing.

Taking a risk, Emma pushed open the front door and led the toddlers outside. She hurried them along the street, towards the Joneses, but Mr Hardshaw suddenly appeared from the back of the carriage, blocking her way, and when she turned round, PC Fossett burst from the front of the house and stopped her retreat.

'Going somewhere?' said Mr Hardshaw.

'Just for a little walk,' said Emma.

'What are you doin' absent from school?' asked PC Fossett

'Mrs Peaseley's gone to the doctor's and I'm to mind the house and bairns.'

'We'd best see you inside then,' said the constable.

Crestfallen, Emma led the way back into the house and showed them into the parlour. She gave the children some bread to eat in the kitchen. PC Fossett began his interrogation, looking at her suspiciously.

'Miss Peaseley, do you always wear them specs?'

'They help me see better.'

'All right, do you know where your brother Alfred is?'

'No, I haven't seen him for a day or two.'

'You must tell me the truth now. It's a matter of life or death. In the early hours of this morning, young

Luke Hardshaw went and got kidnapped.'

Emma's head whirled round and she sank onto a chair, but Mr Hardshaw had no sympathy.

'Listen here, young lady. Yesterday you made an illegal entry into Byrom Hall, pretending to visit my son. As well as trying to steal my vase, you found out where Luke's bedroom was and helped the kidnappers, didn't you?'

'I had nowt to do with it,' said Emma. 'Where's Luke?'

'You should know,' said Mr Hardshaw. 'You and your friend Annie Jones. She went missing at the same time, and you're very friendly with the Joneses, so Madame Renoir tells me. I always suspected a spy at Byrom Hall, ever since a few ideas of mine were stolen. But now they're after the big one. Recognise this?'

Mr Hardshaw pulled a letter from his waistcoat pocket and waved it angrily in front of Emma's face, before reading it aloud.

Hand over your plans for the Self-Rejuvenating Tank Furnace and we will spare your son. Leave them in the ruined malt kiln by the Old Brewery. If they are not there by midnight Monday, he will die a horrible death.

'The murderous villains!' exclaimed PC Fossett. 'Who are they?'

'Can't you see, man?' said Mr Hardshaw angrily. 'Some rival glassmaker out to destroy me. It's taken me years to come up with the idea for a new furnace, a continuous supply of molten metal, twenty-four hours a day, and no waiting around for the next firing. If we surrender it to someone else, we'll soon be out of business.'

'But what about Luke?' said Emma.

'He's a confounded nuisance,' said Mr Hardshaw, 'but worth more than any plan. Nobody's going to kill my son. I'll just have to hand over the documents.'

Emma could feel Clayminster crumbling around her. The failure of Hardshaws would mean the end of work for the Peaseleys and many others, but her heart was torn by the fate of Luke, captured by some treacherous killer.

Someone knocked sharply on the front door and made her jump. With her sixpenny spectacles, she looked through the wall and saw Annie Jones and a beefy young man in tailcoat and boots. PC Fossett brought them into the parlour.

'It's my cook and my coachman!' said Mr Hardshaw. 'Arrest them, officer!'

'What's going on, Mr Hardshaw?' asked Annie.

'Don't you know? Last night Master Luke was kidnapped.'

'Oh dearie me, oh saints and sinners!' said Annie, all flushed. 'That was my fault. I shouldn't have left you all.'

'Explain yourself,' said Mr Hardshaw.

'Well, you see, sir, no-one has ever proposed marriage to me before and when Reginald finally did so behind the stables last night, I thought I'd better see a parson straightaway before he changed his mind. We planned to be back in time to tell you everything, but we had a drink too many to celebrate our engagement. Reginald's mother put us up and I'd just come to tell my own family when I saw your carriage.'

As he listened to her story, Mr Hardshaw's grim face relaxed a little. 'Annie, you've been a good cook to us, and your Lancashire hot-pot allows me to forgive you almost anything.'

'Oh, thank you, sir.'

'Are you married yet?'

'Oh, no, sir, my dad insists it'll have to be the Welsh chapel, and Reginald will have to learn Welsh.'

At this, Reginald's cheery face turned sour, as if he'd tasted a grub-infested apple. Mr Hardshaw allowed himself a little smile.

'That will keep Reginald busy. Now, we shall have to take this young lady to the police station.'

'No,' said Emma, whose temper was up. 'I've got to look after the bairns.'

'Annie can stay here and take care of them,' said Mr Hardshaw.

'What's she done wrong, sir?' said Annie. 'She's only a lass.'

'She's an accessory before the fact,' said Mr Hardshaw. 'From what the constable tells me, this house is a hotbed of conspiracy. There's Alfred Peaseley for a start, but even John Peaseley may be involved. I can't trust anyone. Officer, you'd better report to the superintendent and ask him to prepare the whole force for action.'

'Sir, we have twenty brave men and true,' said PC Fossett, 'and on our new penny-farthings, no-one can resist us.'

Emma took off the spectacles and cleaned them furiously on her pinafore. They accused her of helping criminals kidnap a friend, and now they wanted to blacken the good name of John Peaseley. She put the spectacles back on again and looked through the parlour wall. PC Fossett had left the front door ajar. Her muscles tensed and she leant forward on her chair.

'John's not a kidnapper,' she shouted, 'and you've got it all wrong about me!'

She leapt out of the room and scampered through the front door like a terrier chasing a rabbit. Mr Hardshaw, who was a little overweight, bellowed for PC Fossett to catch her, but when the bobby tried to get into the hallway, Annie blocked his way, and they danced from side to side, like two people who meet on a pavement and can't decide which way to go. Finally PC Fossett pushed her aside.

''Ere, you can't do that!' said Reginald, in defence of his loved one.

Annie's action helped Emma flee round the corner of Clarence Street before the constable could blow his whistle. She crossed Victoria Road, sprinted towards the Canal Bridge, and was soon out of sight.

Chapter 11
Glass Fish

Just before the Market Place, Emma stopped for a breather and wondered what to do next. She couldn't get Luke out of her mind. Where was he now, shivering in some damp dark cellar? Finding him would be well nigh impossible amid the thousands of buildings in Clayminster, but she had to try, for his sake and for everybody else's. She would use her sixpenny spectacles, as best she could.

If Alfred were the kidnapper, where would he choose to hide? His favourite haunts were public houses, but what did Mrs Jones say, a hundred and sixty of them in the town?

She trawled around the Market Place and gazed through the brick walls of taverns with a bewildering array of animal names, *The Black Horse, The Spread-Eagle, The Pig and Whistle* and *The Three-legged Mule.* She looked through tap rooms and lounges, down into cellars, and into upper rooms, often shocked by what she saw, but determined to find Luke.

A pair of policeman appeared on penny farthings, and Emma had to dodge away. In running across Market Street, she dropped the spectacles, and a horse and cart crunched them into little splinters.

Emma slumped on the kerb, feeling broken and

shattered like the glass on the road. Her only weapon had been lost, and now she would never find Luke. What else could she do, but surrender to the police? She sank her head in her hands.

The cries of the market vendors made her look up. A man was selling glass friggers, like John made. She jumped to her feet and went straight to his stall, where he had all kinds of ornaments, birds, animals, even fish, like the Roman one she'd seen at Byrom Hall.

She picked up a glass fish and asked how much it was.

'Threepence,' said the stall owner.

'Can I pay you to-morrow?' said Emma.

'Not on your nelly,' said the man.

'John Peaseley's my foster-brother. He'll pay you.'

The man smiled. 'I work wi' John. It's young Emma, isn't it? Go on then, I'll see him on my next shift.'

He handed over a glass fish, and Emma thanked him and ran down some back streets to the canal. She crossed the bridge and paused for breath, thinking over her next move. What use was a glass fish going to be? She could have been a cat, or a monkey, or a dog, and maybe sniffed out Luke. But a glass fish? She sat on the canal bank and gazed inside its shining crystal scales, willing it to take her to Luke.

Diamonds twinkled, and in a flash she was inside the fish, turning it into flesh and blood, and slipping into the murky waters of the canal. She felt strange, with no legs or arms, but her tail and fins whipped her along, through a world of green and blue and yellow, and she could smell rotting eggs, the familiar essence of Clayminster.

As she reached the Steamies, where the pet-shop owner had dumped his stock, she was chased by two large tropical fish with rubbery lips and purple and green stripes. By some dazzling manoeuvres, she escaped, and swam along the canal towards the river.

A flat-bottomed barge loomed overhead and a worm was dangling on the end of a line. Emma was tempted to eat the worm. Eat the worm? She would be sick, surely, but her fishiness took over and with a gulp she swallowed it whole. It tasted like tripe, or cow's stomach, a favourite dish in Clayminster. As she smacked her fishy lips together, a sharp pain hit the roof of her mouth and she was hauled through the water, into bright sunlight and hung on the end of the line in terrible agony.

'Well, I've never seen owt like it,' said a familiar voice.

Even in her pain, Emma could tell it was Alfred Peaseley. He clumsily pulled the hook from Emma's mouth and dropped her in a jar of water, where she gulped for oxygen through her gills. Her mouth hurt, but through her bulging eyes she could see the barge was half-filled with coal and moored right out in the country. Two horses, used for towing, were munching grass at the side of the canal.

Alfred went to the end of the barge, and into the cabin. He came out, dragging Luke by the hair, and threw him onto a heap of coal.

'There, have a munch on that, your lordship. See

what it's like to work down a mine and eat coal dust.'

Luke was bedraggled and filthy, his clothes torn and his face scratched and bruised. Emma swam around her jar in desperation. Alfred just laughed, picked up a piece of coal and pushed it into Luke's mouth. The boy was struggling for breath and in her anguish Emma bashed her tail against the sides of her jar.

A tall figure came out of the cabin, and rapped the door frame with a grey parasol. Emma recoiled in shock and did a somersault in the water, as she recognised Madame Renoir, Luke's governess.

'Alfred, desist,' she said, in a cold voice. 'Remember, he's our passport to new glory. We must be patient. I'll let you loose on the town later, when we have the documents.'

'Can I, Madame Renoir?' said Alfred, a mad glint in his eyes. 'I could burn down a few places, poison the water supply, or drop a few bombs.'

'Your bombs have not been effective so far,' said. Madame Renoir.

'That train was just a taster,' said Alfred. 'The start of our workers' revolution.'

'Haven't you seen the light yet, my dim-witted friend?' said Madame Renoir. 'Forget the workers, this is about profits and glory. It's me against the Hardshaws. I killed the best of them, when he refused to help me, and for the last five years I've spied on them, as governess to this nauseating boy. Soon I shall possess their biggest secret – the Self-Rejuvenating Tank Furnace. Ah! Just saying it sends a shiver down my spine!'

'You said we'd get money from the Hardshaws,' said Alfred, 'and go to Russia and fight the Tsar.'

He pulled in his line and looked gloomily at the empty hook. Madame Renoir just laughed, a scornful laugh.

'You British,' she said, 'all dreamers, with your glorious Empire. Well, I shall rule the world with my own empire, an empire of glass. Streets of glass, houses of glass, bridges of glass, and towers of glass, reaching up to the sky. Glass that can withstand bullets, fly through the heavens, or cover the Earth. Forget the Crystal Palace. My palaces will be everywhere!'

'Balderdash!' shouted Luke. 'My father's the best glassmaker!'

Alfred cuffed him roughly about the head, and Emma flicked her tail and swam angrily around her jar.

'There's only one fear I have,' said Madame Renoir. 'I can sense it, even now.'

She came over to the jar and pressed her beak-like nose against it. Her narrow staring eyes looked even nastier through the glass, and Emma shrank to the bottom.

'What is this fish?' she said.

'I don't know,' said Alfred. 'I just caught it. I'll use it as bait for the big ones.'

'I doubt if there are big fish in this canal,' said Madame Renoir. 'They won't grow in the filth, not unless they are freaks with three heads.' She wrinkled her nose. 'Strange. There is a power emanating from this jar.'

'It's the stink of the canal water,' said Alfred.

'What happened to that scruffy little sister of yours, who hung around the Hardshaws?'

'Emma? She's nowt but a serving lass.'

'There was something about her I didn't like. She needs crushing, like this fish.'

Madame Renoir reached into the jar with two bony fingers and was about to pinch Emma and squeeze the life out of her, when Luke suddenly made a dash towards the gangplank. Sneakily, Alfred stuck a foot out and tripped him up.

'He needs a lesson or two,' said Alfred. 'I'll bury him in coal for a while, that should slow him down.'

He dragged Luke towards the coal heap and began to shovel coal over him.

Emma could stand no more of this cruelty and felt herself bursting with anger. Her body lengthened, her head expanded, fingers and arms began to form, and in one mighty explosion of glass and water she burst from the jar and stood there, dripping with water like a monster from the murky canal.

The effect was devastating.

In a panic, Madame Renoir tottered backwards and fell amongst the coal, grovelling and cowering on all fours. Alfred ran for it, all the way down the barge and leapt into the smelly water.

'Quick!' said Emma, and she grabbed Luke's hand.

'Where did you come from?' said Luke, rubbing the coal dust from his eyes.

'Never mind now,' said Emma.

They crossed the gangplank and were about to run for it, when Luke halted and pointed to the horses.

'There's a quicker way,' he said.

'I can't ride,' said Emma.

'Jump up behind me.'

He untied one of the horses, grabbed its mane and hauled himself up. Emma jumped a few times, but couldn't reach so high, until she saw a mound of grass down the path and scrambled onto it. Luke rode up and she easily pulled herself onto the horse's back. The heavy beast broke into a lumbering trot and carried them along the towpath, past other barges and horses.

As they rode by, the bargemen looked up from their work and gave them a rousing cheer. When they reached the speed of a gallop, Emma nearly slipped off the horse's back and had to cling like a limpet to Luke. Soon the fenced path near the glassworks came into view and she could see the vapour rising from the Steamies.

At the canal bridge, they slowed down, to make way for the crowds of glassworkers on their way to the night shift, who laughed and waved at them. Emma could have stayed there forever, high up on that horse, but Luke took hold of its mane and swung himself neatly to the ground. When Emma tried the same, she tumbled backwards, but he was able to break her fall and help her to her feet.

'Thanks, Emma,' he said. 'You saved my life.'

To her astonishment, he kissed her lightly on the

cheek. She didn't know what to do or what to say. Such a display of affection was strange to her, so she just turned away from him, but instantly felt sorry for doing so. He seemed equally embarrassed by what he had done, and hurriedly tied the horse to a post, patting its back.

A shout from the canal path made them both turn round in panic. It was Madame Renoir and Alfred, astride the other barge horse, riding pell-mell along the towpath and scattering people out of their way. At the bridge, Alfred leapt off, still dripping wet from his ducking, and spoke to a group of men coming out of a public house which faced onto the canal.

He pointed angrily at Luke and Emma, and the gang started after them, a ferocious, wild-looking bunch.

Chapter 12

In the Limelight

The two of them ran for it, dodging around people and wagons, along Bridge Street and past the Market Place into the centre of town, where a crowd was forming for the early evening performance at the Royal Theatre. Outside, propped against steps, a bill board declared the programme to be *The Pirates of Penzance, an entirely new and original comic opera by Messrs. W. S. Gilbert & Arthur Sullivan.*

Luke and Emma ducked into the crowd and hid behind the long skirts of some well-dressed women, who were discussing the opera.

'Harriet says it's even better than *HMS Pinafore*,' said one.

'What's it about?' asked another.

'Well, these pirates capture the Major-General's daughters and the policemen come to arrest them and the pirates aren't really pirates and – Ow!'

Luke had trodden on her foot and the woman grabbed him by the sleeve.

'What are you doing here?' she yelled. 'You dirty little ruffian! If you want the sixpenny seats, wait at the other door!'

Just then Alfred's heavy mob came roaring round the corner, and Emma pulled Luke away and along the side of the theatre. They came to an entrance labelled 'Stage Door' and scrambled inside, crouching low as they passed a man at a desk. Some steps led down to a dark room, like a cellar with a very low ceiling.

Luke groaned and stretched out on the floor.

'Are you all right?' asked Emma.

'I'm aching all over,' he said, 'and chewing coal dust.'

As her eyes grew accustomed to the dark, Emma could see boxes and old curtains scattered around the floor. She brought some curtains over for Luke to rest on. Opposite them was a long wall, with gaps between its panels, and as she looked through a chink, a wonderful sight met her eyes, rows and rows of red velvet seats, rising in balconies as high as she could see. A sudden dazzling flash of light made her back away from the wall.

'What's that?' she said

Luke struggled up and peered through the chink. 'Footlights,' he said. 'A big row of gaslights to light up the actors. We must be under the stage'

Soon they could hear the hum and chatter of people entering the auditorium, which started the two of them talking as well, about Luke's capture, in the middle of the night, bundled into a sack and carried out to a carriage, about Emma's escape from Mr Hardshaw, and the shock appearance of Madame Renoir, the cause of all the trouble.

'I knew all along she was evil,' said Luke, 'but you got the better of her. How did you do it? Come on, how did you find me?'

His eyes shone out from coal-covered rims, urging her to speak. Emma dreaded this moment. How could she explain the impossible? Sarah the nanny hadn't believed her, nor had her friend Mary, but of all people, surely Luke would?

'Promise you won't laugh or say I'm loony?'

'I promise.'

She took a deep breath. 'It all started on Friday morning, when I went to the Great Casting Hall and saw John making a glass ship. I came over funny and started seeing things, like in a fever, only for real. Later on, more and more things happened, always with glass.'

She paused, wondering whether to go on.

'What sort of things?' said Luke.

'I don't know how to tell you.'

'Please, Emma.'

'You won't tell anyone? They might think I'm a witch.'

'No, I won't tell. You don't look like a witch to me.'

'It's spooky, though. You must believe me. I can become anything, go any place, till the glass fever leaves me, and then I'm back here. The best part is when I see my mam and dad, except when he fell off the tightrope.'

'What?'

'In your room that time, with those living pictures.'

Luke scratched his head and pulled a face. 'You mean the stereoscope?'

'Don't look like that,' said Emma. 'You wanted me

to tell you, didn't you?'

'Yes, but what happened to-day?'

'Well, I got this glass fish from Clayminster market.'

'Ha! A fishy story!'

'You promised!'

'Sorry, Emma. Go on, please. Tell me about the glass fish.'

'I changed into the fish and swam down the canal. Then Alfred hooked me onto the barge.'

'Strewth! It sounds like *Alice's Adventures in Wonderland*!'

'I know, I know,' she said, 'but Alice was dreaming it all, wasn't she? I'm not asleep, am I? Pinch me.'

He pinched her, rather painfully, and left a dirty thumbprint on her sleeve. She rubbed her arm.

'I didn't mean that hard.'

'Sorry. Go on, tell me some more.'

'That time in the library, when I vanished, Bacchus took me to Rome in his chariot.'

'He took you to Rome in his chariot? Well, it didn't take you long to get back. I thought you'd nipped upstairs to the thunder box.'

'Stop it!' she said, her blood rising. 'You think you know everything, don't you, in your big house, with all your bedrooms and your fancy toys? I'm telling you, Bacchus took me to Rome and I saw my mam.'

'In a glass vase?' said Luke, with a smile. 'Go on then, what else have you done?'

Emma glared at him. She didn't want to boast, but he was forcing her.

'Once I changed into a swan and flew across Clayminster. I could have flown anywhere.'

'Oh yeah? Next thing I know, you'll be telling me you were the Flamingo Woman.'

'All right, what if I was? I went into the Hall of Mirrors and came out like that.'

'Don't lie, she was a freak, ten feet tall.'

'I'll show you who's lying, I'll show you! Is there anything glass in here? Just you wait and see.'

In a mad rage, she scoured the room, and turned over the boxes, but they were just full of rubbish, old hats and wigs and ballet shoes. She threw one of the shoes at Luke and he ducked just in time.

'I thought I could trust you,' she shouted. 'I wanted tell you the truth, but you're no help to me, no help at all! You don't believe a word I'm saying!'

She turned her back on him and he tried to say something, but the sound of loud applause drowned his words. Emma squinted through the gap in the stage wall and saw a man with long black hair and thick sideburns taking his place on a podium. He rapped his stick and a wave of music washed over her, full of catchy melodies and foot-tapping dances.

Slowly her anger subsided, and she turned round to Luke, but he was fast asleep on top of the curtains. He looked so battered and coal-stained, she felt sorry for him, and sorry she'd lost her temper. After all, who would ever believe her story?

Above her, the stage creaked with heavy footsteps and she knew the pirates had arrived when a chorus of men sang *Pour, oh pour the pirate sherry*! The story unfolded, how the soft-hearted pirates set the Major-General free when he told them he was an orphan. What nice pirates, thought Emma. Then the music stopped and the theatre shook with thunderous applause.

Luke woke up with a start. 'It must be the interval,' he said. 'Time to get out. Alfred and his gang should have gone by now.'

'But I won't know how the opera finishes,' said Emma.

'We can't be listening to opera all night,' he said. 'It's like a glass furnace in here.'

'That doesn't bother me,' said Emma, but he was already pushing open the door. Reluctantly, she followed him upstairs. At the top, Luke glanced round the corner and jumped back.

'Some roughnecks,' he said, 'in a group at the stage door. I think one of them may have seen me. Run for it!'

They dashed behind the backcloth of the scenery, with just enough room to squeeze through, and came out on the other side of the stage. Through a doorway, they climbed up some steps and raced down a long corridor, barging through another door and up more stairs.

Soon they could go no higher, and tumbled through a curtain onto a wooden floor with benches. Emma stood up, panting for breath, and went forward to a balustrade. Her eyes widened at the steepness of the view. Rows of red seats plunged downwards and way below, a blue velvet curtain was drawn across the stage, carrying the coat of arms of Clayminster. Gas lamps lit the whole auditorium, and the air was hot and smelly with the fumes.

'We're up in the Gods', whispered Luke.

Before long the audience returned to their seats and the second act of the opera began. The Major-General came on stage, ashamed because he'd lied to the pirates about being an orphan. He still ordered the police against them, and a chorus of funny constables marched on. The sergeant of police, who was shaking in his boots, sang *A Policeman's Lot is not a Happy One.*

A spotlight focused brightly on him, and further along the gallery Emma noticed a man in black clothes moving a lamp with a brilliant flame and following the sergeant's every move.

'It's limelight,' whispered Luke. 'He's burning a piece of lime with jets of gas.'

The pirates entered, full of vengeance because the Major-General had lied to them. Some of them had no costume, but ordinary clothes, with just a handkerchief around their heads as a gesture to piracy. Emma stared at them in disbelief.

'Look,' she said. 'It's Alfred and his gang!'

The policemen sprang forward and shouted for the pirates to surrender. Now the stage was really full, for the constables had also gained new recruits, who wore real Clayminster police helmets, complete with badge.

From their midst strode a familiar figure, shorter than the others, but heavily bearded and full of courage. He shouted at Alfred and prodded him with his truncheon.

Emma nudged Luke. 'Good old PC Fossett!' she said. 'Somebody's tipped him off.'

She was soon to be disappointed, for Alfred and his crew were not the surrendering types. They wrestled PC Fossett to the ground and quickly overcame his fellow officers, pinning them to the stage. The conductor threw down his stick and the audience screamed. Before the orchestra could flee, Alfred leapt into the pit and put a knife to the conductor's throat.

'Nobody move!' he yelled.

Emma gripped the rail of the balustrade, so hard that her knuckles turned white. What could she do? Where was the glass to help her now?

Someone else was joining Alfred. From the wings, a tall figure appeared, dressed like a pirate maid with a skull and crossbones on her hat. Emma recoiled at the sight of Madame Renoir, who carried a cutlass instead of a parasol, and obviously enjoyed her position centre stage. The governess addressed the audience with her cold, penetrating voice.

'Listen to me, people of Clayminster. All we want is the boy Luke Hardshaw and the girl Emma Peaseley. They are helping us in our work. Surrender them and you can go on with your silly opera. Otherwise, the music will finish forever. Here's a little prelude for you.'

She bent down at the edge of the stage and with her cutlass sliced a chunk of hair from the flowing locks of the conductor, who nearly fainted with terror.

The audience froze, and up in the gallery, the man

operating the limelight ran for his life, giving Emma the inspiration she wanted. She scrambled to the lamp and shone it on Madame Renoir, who screwed her eyes against the brightness.

'Who's that?' she shouted. 'Who's up there?'

'It's me,' shouted Emma. 'The guttersnipe. Here's a little light for you!'

In one swift movement, she thrust her hand against the hot glass of the lamp and into the path of the limelight. The burning pain nearly made her pull away, but she gritted her teeth and held on.

Diamonds glittered underneath her skin, and suddenly her flesh changed into dazzling crystal, which increased a hundred times the power of the light. A searing-hot ray hit the hand of Madame Renoir, who dropped her cutlass and fled the stage, screaming with pain. Next Emma turned the beam on Alfred, who staggered backwards with a blistered arm, allowing the conductor to wriggle free and scurry out of the pit.

For a moment, the pirates were confused and off their guard. The policemen took advantage, and laid into their opponents, knocking some unconscious and chasing others into the wings. Two officers grabbed Alfred and clapped him in hand-cuffs.

The audience rose to their feet and cheered. Some looked up to the gallery and waved their programmes. Luke gazed at Emma with a mixture of shock and admiration.

'Wow, Emma!' he said. 'I should have believed you. Is your hand all right?"

She smiled at him, and watched her flesh returning to its normal colour. 'It's a bit like when you pinched me.'

The curtain into the gallery opened and a young woman hurried across to them. She gave Luke an affectionate kiss, saying how relieved she was he was safe, then looked at Emma with tears in her eyes and hugged her in a warm embrace.

'My glass girl,' she said, 'my brave little glass girl!'

Chapter 13

Our Emma

Three months later, the little Welsh chapel was filled to overflowing, for the wedding of Annie Jones and the coachman Reginald. Emma was a guest of honour, sitting near the front on the bride's side. She looked round and saw George, Hetty and the little ones, all in their Sunday best. No other Peaseleys were present

Madge, fed up with the dithering of Robert Jones, had left home for a better paid job in the cotton mills further north. Her brother John had emigrated with Catherine to the United States of America, where they intended to marry. Glassmaking in America was developing fast, and he wanted his own business.

Emma grieved to see him go. In her darkest moments, John had always given her hope, and it was through him that she started her journey in glass. At the railway station, he kissed and hugged her, before giving her a parcel.

'I kept it safe for thee,' he said.

As the train steamed out of Clayminster, she undid the parcel, and smiled through her tears. It was the glass ship he'd made in the Great Casting Hall, still diamond-bright but with new additions, some tiny flags and a funnel to turn it into a steamer, like the one he was sailing on.

Alfred Peaseley and his gang appeared in court before Mr Hardshaw, who committed them to Ravenpool Assizes on charges of public tumult, kidnapping, and attempted murder. He easily persuaded them to shop Madame Renoir, who was arrested on the night ferry to Belgium. Needless to say, the Hardshaws were shocked at the criminal character of their stern governess, who came with such good references and had even signed the pledge.

The emptiness of number 9, Clarence Street, drew George and Hetty Peaseley closer together. Hetty still used patent remedies, but of a less drastic kind, and her colour was a healthier shade.

'I'm taking Dr Roberts' Pink Pills for Pale People,' she told Emma. 'Would you like some?'

'No thanks,' said Emma, who didn't want her face any pinker than it was by nature.

Back in the chapel, Emma's thoughts were interrupted by the sound of *The Wedding March*, played on a small but strident organ. Coming down the aisle was someone else who didn't need pink pills, Annie Jones, transformed from care-worn cook to glowing princess in her white satin wedding dress. Reginald waited on the front row, frantically practising his Welsh from a book. His face lit up at the sight of his bride-to-be, and the book dropped to the floor.

Across the aisle, sat between his mother and father, Luke Hardshaw waved at Emma. He was home for the week-end from his boarding school, and she'd missed his company. She remembered with a smile what he'd said when he left for the start of term.

'I wish you were coming with me. You know, I might even marry you one day. Cousins are allowed to, aren't they? You're not bad, as girls go. We could travel the world together, fighting wolves and bears and robbers, and find lost treasures in ancient tombs!'

From the other side of Luke, Mr Hardshaw smiled across at her, and tugged at his whiskers. His eyes shone with gratitude whenever he looked at Emma. He couldn't thank her enough for finding Luke and defeating Madame Renoir. The Self-Rejuvenating Tank Furnace was up and running, and producing more plate glass than any other competitor.

'Now Hardshaws will be the biggest and best glassmakers in the world,' he told everyone, 'and Clayminster will prosper, all due to our Emma.'

'Our Emma.' It was John Peaseley who used to speak like that, and now Mr Hardshaw could welcome her in the same way, after what Emma discovered on that night of the opera.

When the stage was cleared of villains, the conductor returned, sporting his new hair cut, to receive a standing ovation. He waved his baton and continued the performance to the end, when the policemen made the pirates surrender 'in Queen Victoria's name.'

Emma sat watching with Luke, in the three-shilling sofa seats given them by the management. They laughed when the pirates turned out to be lords of the realm who had 'gone wrong', and the Major-General not only pardoned them, but gave them his daughters in marriage. Sitting next to Luke and

Emma was their new companion, the woman in the gallery, a happy and smiling Sarah Danby.

All that afternoon, on her day off, she'd been trying to find Emma, and by chance had booked into the same performance of the opera. Emma listened to her story on the way home from the theatre, holding tightly onto her hand. Sarah began with her time in the workhouse, eleven years ago.

'I was pregnant and unmarried, and Mrs Birchall, the overseer, almost refused to take me on. She already had thirty women with infants, all claiming relief. When I came back from my spell in the madhouse, she said my baby had died from typhoid fever, and was already buried. For eleven years I mourned my little girl, but you inspired me to go back and question the overseer this morning. Mrs Birchall looked up her records, and broke down in tears, begging my forgiveness. It wasn't my baby that died.'

Emma's heart was pounding fit to burst. 'Then – where is your baby?'

Sarah smiled, that sweet smile. 'You are my baby,' she said. 'You were mistaken for an orphan and forgotten about. So many babies died in the typhoid epidemic, Mrs Birchall thought mine was one of them. It's all there, in the workhouse register, showing your name on the list of orphans.'

'I knew it!' cried Emma, and she flung her arms around her mother, as tightly as she could, in case she vanished again, like a vision in glass. Sarah stroked her hair and kissed her tears away.

'I met your father in Belgium, when I was touring

in a minstrel group. One night he was waiting for me at the stage-door with a bunch of flowers. I thought him the handsomest man in the world. We fell in love and planned to marry, but before he could tell his family, he was shot dead by an assassin.'

A spasm of pain brought Emma to a halt, as if she could feel the bullet tearing through her own flesh. She remembered her anguish as the tightrope walker fell, and the crack of a rifle in the stereoscope.

'Who killed him?'

'I don't know, but they tried to kill me as well. I caught the ferry back to England and wanted to contact his family, but I lost my nerve when I saw how grand they were. After my illness, I worked as a nanny, to be near babies, and finally got a job with them.'

'You mean – with the Hardshaws?'

'Yes. I wanted to see where your father lived and touch the things he'd touched.'

Into Emma's mind flashed a picture of the flowers left around the memorial tree at Byrom Hall. What was the inscription? *Planted in Loving Memory of* – ? She took a leap into the unknown.

'My dad was James Hardshaw? Mr Hardshaw's brother?'

'Without a doubt,' said Sarah. 'I can see him in your eyes and in the colour of your hair.'

A wave of sadness swept though Emma, sadness at the thought of her father murdered by greedy monsters, but pride came fast behind, pride at being a Hardshaw and having his power in her blood. She remembered the image of the man at the chapel window, his wavy copper-coloured hair and handsome face. That was him, she knew it, and at least she'd seen him as he really was.

But who had killed him? The words of Madame Renoir, when she talked about fighting the Hardshaws, came echoing back – *I killed the best of them, when he refused to help me* – and Emma knew her father's murderer.

The police were keen to discover what she'd overheard on the barge, but they couldn't understand how she came to be there. All they found was a small glass fish, which they traced to a market stall. The legend grew, of a girl who swam the canal to save Mr Hardshaw's son and who fired beams of burning light at villains besieging the theatre.

Some claimed it was the miraculous properties of limelight, but however they tried, no-one could make it fiercer than it was on that night. Others said the girl was simply bewitched, but nobody mentioned burning at the stake. Only Luke and Sarah knew the true story, and when Mr Hardshaw heard of it, he said no-one but a child of James could work such wonders with glass.

Emma was invited to stay at Byrom Hall, but mother and daughter wanted a home of their own, to make up for lost time. They gratefully accepted the offer of a house from him, a house in the country where the air was sweeter and Emma could have a bed with a room all to itself.

Sarah was going to be a singer again, and Emma too had fallen in love with the theatre, which seemed like a world of dreams, far removed from the grim factories of Clayminster. Mr Hardshaw delivered a piano to the house, and Emma learnt to sing the popular songs of the day, like *Beautiful Dreamer*. Her biggest fan was Luke, who suggested they could all become the 'Hardshaw Minstrels' and tour the fairgrounds and sea-side resorts. Mrs Hardshaw nearly fainted at the idea.

And now, in the Welsh chapel, Emma was sitting close to her mother while Annie Jones made her marriage vows, and Reginald followed, his Welsh hesitant at first, but growing in confidence. Mrs Jones had been a strict teacher and he daren't get it wrong. After a hymn, they came back down the aisle and the congregation followed them outside.

Charlie Fossett was there, standing proudly on duty and sporting three stripes, a sign of promotion, *for meritorious action against the recent felons*. He was smiling at Sarah, with a knowing smile, and she was turning bright red.

Emma shook her head. Sergeant Fossett was courting her mother! He'd bumped into her on his penny-farthing, when she ran out of the theatre to report on Alfred and his gang.

The sergeant wanted all three of them to emigrate to New Zealand, where you could dig for gold, buy a ranch for next to nothing, and roam free in the fresh, unpolluted air. Emma's vision of the glass ship on its long voyage might come true after all, if Charlie Fossett had his way.

Her eyes were drawn to the windows of the chapel and a tremor ran down her spine. The plain glass had turned into brilliant colours, a vivid green, rich blues, and splashes of yellow, lit by the afternoon sunshine. She hadn't noticed them before. Was her glass fever returning, when she thought it had left her weeks ago?

Just then, Mrs Jones walked past, carrying a bouquet of flowers.

'Do you like our new windows?' she said. 'We all paid money towards them.'

Emma gave a sigh of relief. 'They're beautiful!'

She quickly held her mother's hand and side by side they walked down the cobbled street, following the happy couple to the wedding feast.

THE END